A Hearing
for
Jim Thorpe
AN EXERCISE IN FRUSTRATION

A HEARING FOR JIM THORPE,
An Exercise in Frustration

First Published by Haynes Bridge Publishing (2009)
Johns Creek, GA USA
www.hbpublishing.com

ISBN-10: 0-9822039-0-x
ISBN-13: 978-0-9822039-0-3

Printed in the United States of America

Cover design by Ann Clayton of Abundant Creative
Cover photography: Cumberland County Historical Society, Carlisle, PA

A Hearing
for
Jim Thorpe

AN EXERCISE IN FRUSTRATION

By
Michael L. Sheaffer

Haynes Bridge Publishing, LLC
Johns Creek, Georgia USA
www.hbpublishing.com

DEDICATION

This book is dedicated to my parents,
Milton and Marie Sheaffer,
who did not live to see my book completed.
I am sure they are with me in spirit.

And also to my wife,
Angie,
who has inspired and encouraged me
to write this book.

ACKNOWLEDGEMENTS

There are a number of people I would like to thank for their input into this book. First, my best friend, Stephen Mark. He has been by my side from the very start of this book, giving me advice, even when I did not ask for it.

Most of the research came from the years I was chairperson of "Project Jim Thorpe" for the Carlisle Jaycees. I thank you, the Jaycees that helped with "Project Jim Thorpe" and became lifelong friends.

On the technical side, I want to thank Ann Clayton for her graphic design expertise in designing the cover and the book marketing materials. And to Jerry Bush who was the first to read the manuscript and provide me with comments and encouragement.

Last, but definitely not least, I want to thank Richard Tritt, Photo Curator, at the Cumberland County Historical Society. Richard helped with the selection of the cover photography.

Thank You

FOREWORD

It seems that the heroes of our childhood stay reminiscently with us as we grow. It doesn't matter what they did or who they were, but their legacy lives on in our hearts and can return us to the warm feelings of childhood in an instant. Jim Thorpe was one of those people to me. Growing up in Carlisle, Pennsylvania, home to the Carlisle Indian School where Jim Thorpe spent many of his school years, I was frequently privy to hearing personal and engaging stories about the infamous Jim Thorpe. He was then and still remains a legendary presence for Carlisle. Growing up it was as if his history was part of my own and even as an adult I feel Jim Thorpe is part of my own heritage.

Like many small towns, Carlisle hangs on to the connection it has with Jim Thorpe. Many of his collectibles have been kept on display to ensure that the legacy lives on. The Cumberland County Historical Society, The Hamilton Library in town, and the US Army Military History Research collection all contains fragments from the life and career of Thorpe. Interestingly enough, the Carlisle Barracks is currently a senior army officer's academy and is located at the exact site where the old Carlisle Indian School used to sit. I imagine that, as time goes on, many more young boys will hear the stories of Jim Thorpe and feel a sense of pride and interest in him. I hope I will be able to gently coerce those feelings in others and with pride, spread his good name.

As fate would have it, I did get to see Jim Thorpe in person just once. To me it was as grand an experience as if John Wayne or the president himself had come and shook my hand. In September of 1951, during the world premiere of the Warner Brother's movie, *Jim Thorpe All American*, I caught a brief but memorable glimpse of the man that I truly admired. Unfortunately, it was my first and last time to see him.

On January 26, 1969, I volunteered to head up a committee for the Carlisle Jaycees. The goals of this committee were to have Jim Thorpe reinstated as the winner of the 1912 Olympic Pentathlon and Decathlon event. The effort was called "Project Jim Thorpe" and I spent three years gathering research, collecting facts, and finding out the truths behind why Jim Thorpe was removed as the winner of these 1912 Olympic events. During this time, my interest in Jim Thorpe came to an all-time peak, and I was somehow reunited with the boy in my past and learning to respect a childhood hero all over again.

Perhaps my favorite boyhood memory is a story I heard about Jim Thorpe. The story unfolds as the coach from the Harrisburg, PA, rival school awaited the Carlisle Indian School bus to arrive for the up-coming track meet. As the bus arrived, the hosting coach expected to greet the whole team, but was surprised to find that only three people exited the bus. The first was the Carlisle coach, "Pop" Warner, the second was Louis Tewanima, and the last was Jim Thorpe. Puzzled, the other coach quickly asked "Pop" where the rest of the team was. Coach Warner smiled coyly and said, "*This is the team. Louis does all the running and Jim does everything else.*" The perplexed other coach probably thought his team would win the match hands down. It turns out that the Carlisle Indian School swept the meet and legend says that Jim Thorpe ran the eighteen miles back to Carlisle after the track meet had ended!

It is no accident that I am the one to offer all the facts about Jim Thorpe in this riveting book entitled "A Hearing for Jim Thorpe, an Exercise in Frustration." It seems that I have spent a lifetime unfolding the story so that the pride and interest I feel in this childhood hero can be shared with the rest of the world.

Michael L. Sheaffer

CHAPTER 1

It is a hot, dry day when I arrive in Carlisle, on the 4:05 PM train from Harrisburg. The dry air is such a contrast to what I'm feeling. After the train ride, I'm far from dry. The telltale signs are my wadded up sopping handkerchief, and, well okay, the darkness under the armpits of my shirtsleeves stretching half way to my waist. I'm feeling conspicuous and guess that I could just put my jacket back on, but temperatures are in the 90s, and with the air so stiflingly still, it feels more like 100 degrees. What do you expect in Pennsylvania in mid-July?

Train 27 is the most direct route, mercifully making only one stop in Mechanicsburg before lumbering into the Cumberland Valley Railroad station on High Street, between Hanover and Pitt Street. As the locomotive grinds to a halt, I notice the *"Cigars, Shines, and Billiards"* sign in a shop window across the way and make a quick pit stop to pick up some stogies. I'd smoked my last one during the miserable train ride and want to thoroughly enjoy my next one in style and after I've had a chance to freshen up.

I'm anxious to get to the comforts of my hotel room. And I do mean comforts. The company spared no expense putting me up in the prestigious Molly Pitcher Hotel. I'll tell you, this was a surprise. It might be a surprise for the boss when he sees the bill. In addition to luxury accommodations, the Molly Pitcher has the added benefit of being located conveniently across from the courthouse, my new, albeit temporary, work environment. At least I won't be dripping with sweat from a long walk under a blazing sun, though the sure-to-be-crowded surroundings I'll be working in will certainly take care of that.

As eager as I am to get to the finest hotel in town, wash away that train ride in style, and peruse the menu of that famed dining room, I make a stop at the Cumberland County Courthouse, to get the lay of the land. I'm going to need it.

I'm here, by the way, to cover a story, the biggest sports story of the year. It's not taking place on any ball field, but right here inside this building. More like a battlefield. Actually, one of the sandstone columns of the Cumberland County Courthouse still exhibits the battle wounds of artillery shelling that ultimately preceded the Battle of Gettysburg in 1863. Yeah, I'd say this is an appropriate setting for what's about to take place.

Beginning tomorrow, the whole world will be reading about why Jim Thorpe, one of the most revered athletes of our time, has been stripped of his Olympic medals and titles. One by one, the facts leading up to these events will be revealed at a media-spectacle courthouse hearing and a judge will decide whether Thorpe's medals should be returned to him.

As the sports reporter for the *Evening News*, I'll be among those media hounds. The name is Bud Murphy, and this could well be the biggest story of my career. Well, maybe that's just wishful thinking. Much as I hate to say it, maybe the big story's already been told, broke by the damned *Worcester Telegram*. What can happen here but a mere recounting of the facts that led to the removal of those medals? The committee sure as hell wouldn't have done some thing that drastic, that final, and well, cruel, without cold, hard proof. But something about this whole thing still nags, or maybe that's *gnaws*, at me.

I fight my gut instincts and focus on the facts. Isn't this what a reporter's supposed to do? The Olympics are for amateur athletes, as in athletes who don't get paid for what they do. It was uncovered that Thorpe had been paid as an athlete prior to his amazing Olympic performances and medals. Ya gotta admit, the guy is beyond belief. No amateur or professional has ever accomplished what he did, and it's hard to believe anyone else ever will. But the rules are the rules. That's the way I see it. And I guess that's the way the Olympic Committee saw it when they took away his awards.

I'm not so sure that's the way the residents of Carlisle see it, though. Since Thorpe's a local boy who's much loved by the folks here, I am pretty sure that the courtroom will be packed with supporters tomorrow. Ought to be interesting.

Staring at the shelled column and impressive bell tower of the courthouse, I envision the proud defenders of Carlisle back in 1863, as General Stuart and his army paused briefly here during the Gettysburg campaign of the American Civil War. Though not a significant battle in and of itself, the skirmish here detained Stuart's troops in their rendezvous with General Lee at Gettysburg. Their arrival well into the second day of battle could well have shaped the course of history and life as we know it today. God knows where this country would be now had Gettysburg been lost.

I wonder if the citizens of Carlisle will rally to the defense of their native son with as much courage and character; and I can't help but wonder if the events that transpire here will amount to more than restoring some prize. If, like the Battle of Carlisle, there's more at stake that we may not even comprehend in this moment. History has a way of doing that. Not making its significance immediately known to those who live it, but sending an ever-lasting message for generations to come. What lessons will we not fully grasp at the end of this historic hearing? What lasting impact will the results have on future generations?

"Screw your head back on, Murphy," I say to myself. At least, I hope I said it to myself. I can get carried away and make something out of nothing like nobody's business. Maybe that's why I became a reporter.

In any case, it's not my job to speculate about the longstanding importance of the Thorpe hearing. My job is to report the facts that will be revealed in this building tomorrow.

I'd like to see the layout before I have to fight my way through the crowd in the morning, so I'm heading to the second floor hearing room for a look around.

The room probably holds two hundred people comfortably, maybe five or six to each white-painted wooden row. The half dozen extra-long windows are closed now, since there's nothing happening here today. The courtroom is almost eerily quiet, populated only by the ghosts of past witnesses, of decisions that tried to serve justice and probably broke many hearts, and of people like me, who depend on the victories and defeats of others to earn their bread and butter.

In truth, though, I am a little out of my element here. The triumphs and trouncings I write about aren't nearly as solemn and significant as the judgments handed down in this building. But, in the Jim Thorpe case, in the interest of fair play and for the good of the game the findings here could impact sports – both amateur and professional, and possibly even my career, in a major way.

I nudge personal ambition aside and wonder what the judge will be like. Once he enters the courtroom from that side door and takes his place behind the imposing oak bench, he'll be running the show. It'll be just the judge at the bench, and his clerk at the small table beside it. The jury seats to the left of the bench will be empty, since this isn't a trial. Can't help but wonder whether that's good or bad for Thorpe – his peers would probably give him back the medals in a minute, which is probably about how much time the Olympic Committee took to strip him of them—but who knows what the judge will decide?

So it looks like this historic old building is about to acquire another piece of history. I've already seen the battle scars on the column outside. I wonder what sorts of scars this room will bear once the sides retire. I have no doubt that many will be buried in deep, invisible places, like in the heart and on the soul.

Leaving the courthouse, I walk the half block to the Molly Pitcher on South Hanover Street. The hotel's reputation precedes it—everyone who heard I'd be staying here envied me my good fortune. As the doorman opens the polished oak door and I step into the lobby, without thinking I find myself letting out a low whistle. From the elegant mahogany front desk to the inlaid marble floor, the place is awash in luxury.

The uniformed clerk looks up as I approach the desk.

"Good afternoon, sir. Welcome to the Molly Pitcher Hotel. My name is Jimmy. How may I help you?"

I tell him I'm checking in and give him my name. When he sees that my room will be paid for by the newspaper, he asks if I'm in town on business.

"Yes, as a matter of fact I am," I say, intending to merely respond to his question. Truthfully, I am not at all interested in a conversation at the moment. I want to get to my luxury digs, literally peel the clothes off my back and clean up. I can't wait to grab some dinner. My stomach's grumbling, especially since I'm about to fill it with fine dining. My plan is to buy the most expensive damned thing on the menu. But I find myself adding, "I'm a sports reporter for the *Evening News*, and I'll be covering the Jim Thorpe hearing for the paper. I guess the town's pretty excited about it."

"You have no idea, Mr. Murphy," Jimmy replies. "Most everyone in Carlisle and the nearby towns loves Jim Thorpe and we all think it's a shame the way his medals were taken away. I say he earned them fair and square, if you don't mind my opinion."

I actually do mind, a little. But I'm a good enough reporter to know when an opportunity presents itself, so I satisfy my appetite for information first.

"Not at all, Jimmy," I say. "I'm as interested in what the folks of Carlisle think as I am in what's going to happen in that courtroom. I figured most people here would be on Thorpe's side."

Jimmy seems to consider this comment for a moment before he responds. "Well sir, Carlisle is a patriotic place. George Washington has come through this town; Ben Franklin too. And the local Carlisle Indian School Cadets took part in President Teddy Roosevelt's special inauguration parade just ten years ago. That sure was a proud day! And of course there's Molly herself." He's referring to the hotel's namesake, the legendary Molly Pitcher, the only woman buried here with other veterans of the Revolution who fought right along with the men in the Revolutionary War. "Folklore has it that she came by the name by carrying pitchers of water to soldiers manning their cannons on the battlefield. The water wasn't even for the soldiers to drink, although I'm sure Molly took care of them too. The water was needed to swab the cannons."

Jimmy is turning out to be a real historian. He certainly knows his stuff. Just as I'm beginning to wonder where this little history lesson is headed, he continues, "Anyway, what I mean is that Jim Thorpe is an American Indian, and he represented this country in the Olympics and won those races. And it just seems unpatriotic to me and lots of others that anybody can say he didn't. A fact's a fact, is what I'm saying."

Naturally, the residents of Carlisle are behind their hometown hero. I want to point out to Jimmy that these aren't the only facts, but something about his passion for history and ardor for Thorpe gives me pause—that, and the voice that booms behind me.

"Sure is, Son." I turn to see a powerfully built man in his mid-forties approaching from across the lobby. He puts out his hand. "Glenn Warner," he says. "Call me Pop."

Now, you don't have to be a sports reporter to know who Pop Warner is. But, because I *am* a sports reporter, I am humbled, honored, and nervous as heck in his presence. "It's an honor to meet you, Mr. Warner," I nearly stammer, shaking the hand of this living legend, at least in my book. This is quickly becoming about the luckiest day of my life.

In my dozen or so years on the sports beat, I've covered much of the famed coach's impressive football career. Pop Warner is always news. He began as a player for Cornell University in the early 1890s, and got the nickname "Pop" because he was older than most of his teammates. The name stuck. Although he graduated with a law degree, he went to work for the University of Georgia as its football coach. The place had no athletic facilities, no playing field, no stands for the spectators. No players, either, but somehow after only two years, Pop gave Georgia its first undefeated season. His team at the University of Pittsburgh went undefeated last year, too. What this guy can do for a football team is nothing short of unbelievable.

I knew he coached when Thorpe first arrived at the Carlisle Indian School, so I figured him to be a key player at the hearing. I didn't figure I'd be meeting him face to face in the lobby of my hotel.

"I couldn't help but overhear that you're here to cover Jim Thorpe's hearing," Pop says, eyeing my bags and briefcase.

I'm wondering if he views me as friend or foe? I would have preferred meeting the guy after one of his victorious, undefeated football seasons, writing glowing accounts of his genius and the talents of his players. Instead, here I am reporting on the fall from grace—I mean impending fall from grace—of one of his former star players. I'm not so sure I would like me, either.

"I'll be testifying for Jim, of course," Warner continues. "I have to agree with our man here that a fact's a fact, alright, and Thorpe deserves to have those medals back. Damn shame what those idiots did to his good name."

I am suddenly very grateful for the impromptu history lesson from my favorite desk clerk, Jimmy. Without it, what came next simply wouldn't have happened.

"Listen," Warner continues, "I'm waiting for my dinner companion. I'm dining with Moses Friedman. He was the superintendent over at the Indian School when Jim was a student. That's where I coached him. Why don't you join us and we can tell you a little bit about Jim. I'm sure Moses would be pleased to meet you."

Well, he doesn't appear to view me as a foe. This is an incredible stroke of luck. Just a short while ago, I was eyeing prime seating in the courtroom, angling for the best access to key witnesses, hoping to catch an off-the-record comment or ask a perspective-altering question that would set my story apart from the rest. I had that gut feeling again, the one where my reporter's nose starts to twitch as it senses a scoop. I've had it before, though it didn't work out quite so well. This could be the break I've been waiting for. What better background for my story could I find than Thorpe's coach and friend? And what a coach.

"I can't think of a more enjoyable way to spend my first night in Carlisle. I'd love to join you, Mr. Warner," I reply with more expression than I mean to. But I can't help it. Dinner at the Molly Pitcher with Pop Warner was about as close to rubbing elbows with high-society as I have ever or will ever come. It looks like my sports story might end up with that human interest spin I've been thinking about, and this really just might be the story of my career.

"I'm just going to run up to my room and clean up if you don't mind." I gesture to my rumpled clothing. "Been traveling in these for hours." As anxious as I had been to get to my room, I am now reluctant to leave the company of Pop Warner. "We'll wait on you, son. Take your time. Moses and I have plenty to catch up on," he says amicably. "What's your name anyway, bud?"

I look at him, startled at first. How the heck does he know my name? And then, my brain starts working again. "Actually, Mr. Warner, the name is Bud. Bud Murphy."

He laughs, a genuine one right from the gut. "Call me Pop, Bud."

As Jimmy rings for the bellhop to carry my bags to my room, I slip a couple of slightly rumpled and damp bills into his unsuspecting hand.

CHAPTER 2

After accepting Glenn Warner's dinner invitation, I follow the bellhop into room 310, at the front of the building overlooking Hanover Street. The pale yellow walls are warmed by the sun filtering through the sheer white curtains that gently blow in the warm breeze. A green chenille spread covers the double bed, which looks welcoming and soft. I didn't realize that I was so tired but that comfortable bed is going to have to wait.

I quickly wash up at the basin then change my shirt and tie, put on a fresh jacket, and leave the rest of the unpacking for later. I wipe the dust from my shoes, brush my damp hair, take a quick glance in the mirror to make sure I'm reasonably presentable, and then head downstairs.

Not seeing Warner in the lobby, I figure that he has already been seated in the dining room. As I enter the dining room through the oak-mullioned glass doors, the sumptuous aromas of roasting beef and fresh baked goods remind me that I'd had a very light lunch when the train stopped in Mechanicsburg earlier today. I kept it light anticipating what the Molly Pitcher would offer. The meal I have long awaited beckons, as I ask the maitre d' for Mr. Warner's table and am escorted to a comfortable corner where Warner and another man are seated at a table for four.

Warner rises and shakes my hand, saying, "Glad you could join us. Meet Moses Friedman, superintendent of the Carlisle Indian School. Moses, meet Bud Murphy, sports reporter for the *Evening News*."

The other man rises as well and extends his hand. He appears to be about fifty, thin in comparison to Warner's athletic build, with a quick smile and warm brown eyes.

"Glenn's told me about your assignment," Friedman says. "I'm sure between us we can give you plenty of background for your story. I think it's just as important to know the facts behind the man as it is to report the facts about his case, don't you?" he asks. I would have nodded yes, whether I agreed with him or not. But, the truth is, I did agree.

We settle on first names all around, and proceed to each order an Iron City lager from our waiter. Our drinks soon arrive in frosted mugs and we all fall silent as we take the first refreshing sips. I can't remember the last time something tasted so good. This evening can't get much better.

Looking around the room, I realize that everything I've heard about the Molly Pitcher's reputation has to be true. The dining room is beautifully appointed. Oak panels rise midway up the walls, which are painted a warm hunter green that lends the room a masculine yet comforting feel. The pine tables are formally set with fine china and heavy silver on crisply ironed white cloths. The dark oak floor is intermittently decorated with fine oriental rugs, and several sparkling crystal chandeliers hang throughout the room. The patrons are elegantly dressed in formal dinner attire and most of the women wear exquisite jewels.

As we study our menus, I'm having a hard time focusing. I still can't believe that I am having dinner with the great "Pop" Warner. What I want almost more than anything is to interview him but think I'd better wait until after dinner when we're having coffee before I ask about his career. Anyway, Pop wants to talk about Thorpe and this is what I need for the story I'm reporting on right now. Even though I know most of the stories about Pop, I'd love to hear him tell them personally. Who knows, with this lucky cloud that I've managed to walk under, I may get the chance to do both. I order a Delmonico steak and baked potato, Warner selects double-cut pork chops, and Friedman settles on roasted chicken. Once we've placed our orders, we begin to relax a bit and our conversation turns to talk about Jim Thorpe.

Warner begins by filling me in on the facts of Thorpe's early life. Jim had a twin brother named Charlie and they were born in Oklahoma in 1887, to parents who were both of mixed descent. He was raised as a Sac and Fox and attended the Sac and Fox Indian Agency School in Stroud, Oklahoma. When the boys were eight years old, Charlie died of pneumonia. This was an event that Jim could not handle well. Jim struggled with dealing with Charlie's death, and he ran away from school several times until his father sent him to the Haskell Indian National University in Lawrence, Kansas, to keep him from running away again. Just as Jim was starting to adjust and cope with Charlie's death, two years later his mother died. Thorpe became very depressed and eventually ran away from home to work on a horse ranch.

In 1904, at age 17, Jim returned to his father and decided to join the Carlisle Indian Industrial School in Carlisle. It was here that he met Glenn Warner. When Jim's father died later that year, the boy again left school and resumed farm work, but returned to Carlisle three years later, which is when his athletic achievements began.

"Hard to lose as much as that young man did at such an early age," Warner shakes his head sadly. "Without the Indian School, who knows what might have become of him?"

Before continuing the story about Jim, both Friedman and Warner agree that understanding the Indian School is an important step in understanding Jim Thorpe and that Friedman is a wealth of knowledge on this subject. Friedman explains that the school was founded in 1879 by Richard Henry Pratt, an army field officer whose military experiences led him to believe that Indians must be taught to reject tribal culture and adapt to white society to save them from extinction.

Pratt chose the town of Carlisle as the site for his school for a number of reasons. The town was far enough west that the students would not be confused by city life. It was also far enough away from the reservations that the boys wouldn't be able to run away back to their homes. Vacant army barracks in town would serve well as student dormitories and the dorms were only two miles from Dickinson College, a well-established school.

As I listen to the history, I keep trying to picture those Indian boys, taken away from their families, scared out of their minds, not knowing what would happen to them. Friedman tells me that when the first group of students arrived in Carlisle, they were wearing their tribal outfits and singing Indian songs. Townspeople lined up at the train station to see them and had a grand time watching the show, not even thinking about how frightened the kids might be.

But the people of Carlisle meant no harm to the boys, and came to love the Indian School students. They quickly learned that these Indian boys were just like the town boys who would rather tease each other and have a good game of ball than dance to drums and cymbals. Funny how that's how it usually works out. Pratt's ultimate goal to turn the Indian youth into productive Americans appeared to work well for everyone. Students were taught the English language and prohibited from speaking any other within the school environment. Pratt kept close contact with his staff and students and held regular sessions about topics that included religious and moral themes. He employed dedicated teachers and followed the lives of his students even after they departed the school.

The people of Carlisle became particularly enamored of the Indian students' athletic prowess, especially the football team. Games between the school's Carlisle Indians and Dickinson College's Red and White drew huge crowds. At times, more than ten thousand fans filled the stands, which was a frequent occurrence when Jim Thorpe played. During one of these games, they beat Dickinson 34-0, with Thorpe running a bad punt snap for 105 yards and the score. Although the crowds cheered for both teams, the Indians were usually the favorites when they traveled to other cities. In fact, in 1912, they were the highest scoring team in the nation.

The Indian students and their football team became so popular that they even received special treatment from the Carlisle police. Although the Indian School had banned the use of alcohol, players sometimes received some from fans.

At this point in the story, Warner grins impishly. "Sometimes I was their biggest fan," he says.

"You gave them booze?" I ask, surprised.

Warner laughs. "Yeah, on occasion. Those fellows worked hard and deserved a little fun every now and then. A few times, a boy would go a little overboard and get in some trouble with the cops. But the police would always call me and I'd bail the kid out. Nobody ever got hurt."

The team was such a huge draw that powerhouse schools like Yale and Harvard paid the Carlisle Indian School purses as high as $15,000 for a single game. The school used this money to provide perks for the team and to enhance other aspects of the school. Eventually, the Carlisle Indians became the first big business team in college football history.

"And that," says Friedman, "is how our friend here got to be their coach. The team was doing so much good for the school that Pratt felt that improving their performance would only add to their attraction. That's when he hired Pop to coach those boys to glory.

"The problem with Pratt was that he did not see the value of sustaining the traditions and beliefs of the Indian culture," Friedman continues. "The students rallied for change, and that's when I became the new superintendent. I believe we were much more open-minded."

"When a school gets such a magnificent reputation and the people who are laboring within its gates are satisfied and conclude that it has reached the climax of usefulness and cannot be improved, then something, somewhere is radically wrong," Moses seems to recite. "I spoke those very words, or something very similar, at the Lake Mohonk Conference back in 1908, and I still believe them to be true today," he adds with a smile.

By now we've finished our meal and ordered coffee and apple pie. I ask Warner how he'd liked coaching the Indian School team in comparison to the other teams he's worked with.

"I loved those boys," he says with feeling. "I've enjoyed every team I've coached, but the Indian students had so many other things to deal with, like being away from their families and learning a whole new way of life. Their determination really impressed me and they seemed so happy to be considered an important part of the town."

As I listen to Warner, I realize how appropriate the nickname "Pop" really is. Football is only one of the things he wants to teach his teams. This is a man who believes in the boys he coaches and who appreciates the role that sports can play in developing character. From what I've learned tonight about the Indian students, I think Warner must have been the perfect man to work with those scared, uncertain kids. He really was like a father to so many of them, a role he seems to take very seriously.

Pop is drumming his fingers on the table, staring at me intently, as if he's trying to decide whether he should say something. We've managed to get through our entire meal and dessert without one solid mention of the reasons we're all here. I think it's probably best to keep it that way. Moses, whose role in the lives of the Indian students was just as significant as Pop's, shifts in his seat. "The Indian School may not be what it was when Pop and I were there, but it still has value and merit. Though, maybe not much of a football team, anymore," he laughs. "Remember the first time they beat Harvard, Pop? That was sure a game to remember!"

Pop's eyes twinkle, maybe even glisten up a bit, at the memory. "Jim was our running back, defensive back, place-kicker, and punter," he recalls. "He scored every point in that game. Four field goals and a touchdown. I'm sure, as a seasoned sports reporter, this is old news to you, Bud. You'll have to forgive me and Moses on our walk down memory lane. Those were some special days for us—and for Jim."

"They were special for any true sports fan, Pop," I agree. I mean, who does that kind of thing? Thorpe's performances, even then, were the stuff of legend. "What are some of your other favorite memories?" I ask them both. This is better conversation than I could have hoped for and much safer than the unpleasant realities of the present.

"The Army game," they say in unison. "We whipped 'em, 27-6. Jim scored a ninety-two-yard touch down that was called back because of a penalty. So, on the very next play, what does he do? Runs one back for a ninety-seven-yard score. He was voted All-American for the second year in a row" Moses says proudly. "One of their guys on Army was pretty good, I remember," Pop chimes in. "He hurt his knee pretty badly trying to tackle Jim. Never quite the same after that. Poor guy. He had a future. Dwight Eisenhower, I think his name was. Wonder what became of him?" You could tell the guy cared about not only his players, but players and the sport in general.

There is another thing I'm very curious about and I ask Warner, "Pop, what made you choose football over a career in law? It couldn't have been easy to finish a law degree and still be such a terrific player. Was it a hard decision?"

He takes a sip of his coffee and carefully puts the cup back on its saucer. "Bud, I have great respect for the law and thought it would be a fine career. My mind's always been pretty logical. I liked to study and I can be plenty persuasive, so I thought it was a good fit. But when I was playing at Cornell, it occurred to me that all those things applied to football too. You have to be able to think logically to plan plays, you have to study those plays and the other teams' moves, and being team captain involved a good deal of persuasion, too."

I nod, fascinated by this line of thinking. I could listen to this man all night.

"It started to dawn on me that I had a choice," Warner continues. "I could become a lawyer and spend my days working alone in a library and trying cases in a stuffy courtroom, or I could stay with football and spend my days outdoors, as part of a team, teaching younger fellows the value of honest competition."

Honest competition? A part of me wants to interject here, ask him if he thinks what Thorpe did was "honest" competition. Was it honest to compete in the Olympics when he had been paid to play a sport? Could Warner have known about it all along, I wonder. I shake the questions from my skeptical reporter mind and focus on the here and now. I am sitting in the Molly Pitcher, dining and shooting the breeze with Pop Warner. Tomorrow, I'll be the cynic. Tonight, I am a fan.

"So it was really coaching that you knew you wanted to pursue?" I ask.

"Absolutely. The way I see it, the youth who doesn't thrill to the strain of struggle and the joy of victory isn't much of a lad. I felt that if I could help young men to succeed on the football field, what they learned from that might help make them better at whatever they choose to do in their lives."

By now it's after 9:00. As much as I hate for this remarkable evening to end, I am exhausted, and I don't want to impose on Warner and Friedman any longer. They've been tremendously open and helpful and I thank them both as Pop insists on paying the dinner check.

We leave the dining room together, say goodnight, and head to our rooms. Although I'm bone tired, I take a pad and pencil from my battered leather briefcase and sit at the small desk near the window. Looking across at the courthouse, I light that cigar I bought earlier and begin to make some notes for my story, while the dinner conversation with Warner and Friedman is still fresh in my mind.

My story. Now, that's a laugh. My mind starts wandering, back to the morning two-and-a-half years ago when my editor slapped a copy of *The Worcester Telegram* on my desk. "Thorpe with professional baseball team, says Clancy," was the headline that screamed up at me.

"What in hell is this?" my boss demanded. As his florid face grew even more red with anger, I became paler by the second. I could barely breathe. Charles Clancy, manager of the Winston-Salem baseball team in the Carolina League, claimed that Jim Thorpe had played professional ball for him in 1910, two years prior to competing in the Olympics.

My head was spinning and not because of the news. I'd been talking to Clancy, preparing to run this same story in *The Providence Times*, where'd I'd been the sports reporter for three years. I wasn't fully comfortable that I had all the facts and was still doing some research before going to print. I checked the byline. Roy R. Johnson. I hadn't known Clancy was talking to another reporter and wondered if Johnson had any more facts than I did, or just went for the breaking news.

And to be honest, being scooped on this one really hurt. I'd hoped that this story would be my ticket to the big leagues. Providence was a good town and a decent paper, but I'd had my eye on a bigger city, maybe Boston or Philly, where I hoped to really make a name for myself.

I'd barely been thirty when the Thorpe story broke and was convinced that my career was over. Actually, my editor, Fred Delaney, was so mad that the *Times* lost the story that he repeatedly told me I'd never get anywhere. Reporters can stay in their careers until they're old and gray—I probably have plenty of time left to hit it big. But Fred's attitude never improved much, and working for him became impossible. He'd make bets with other reporters on whether I'd be scooped on whatever story I was following. He barely acknowledged my work and, after about six months, I couldn't stand it any longer.

I'd started nosing around the Boston papers, but no one was in the market for a new sports reporter. Then it hit me that maybe I should get out of New England altogether. Between the *Worcester Telegram* and the *Providence Times*, I thought a change of scenery might be in order.

So I took a chance. I packed up my things and got on a train to Philadelphia, sight unseen. I rented a room downtown and hit the bricks every day, checking all the dailies for work. No one was hiring, but I met a nice fellow named Pete Wilson at the *Philadelphia Press* who took a liking to me. We had a couple of beers together, and he told me about an editor in Harrisburg who was looking for someone to cover sports. He even wrote a letter of introduction for me.

I figured taking one more chance couldn't hurt. I bought another train ticket and traveled 120 miles west to Harrisburg, where I've been for the last two years. The man who hired me at the *Evening News*, Jack O'Brien, is a good man and a fair editor. So far, I like my job well enough, and I was certainly glad when Jack assigned me to cover this hearing.

Honestly, Harrisburg isn't a bad place to write about sports. The city got its first baseball club in '01, and for the last two years, the Senators won the Tri-State Association championship. In fact, it looks like they might make it a triple this year. Pretty good stuff for the minors. And just this spring, the International League Newark Indians moved to Harrisburg. A lot of people were surprised that a Triple-A team made the move, and I've been hearing some rumors that they might not stay more than one season. It'll be hard to lose a good team, especially in my line of work. If it happens, I sure hope it won't mean getting on another train to who-knows-where.

Coming back to reality, I see that I've finished my cigar without even being aware of smoking it. All this hindsight will get me nowhere, and there's no point dwelling on what I can't change. I lost the Thorpe story once, and I'll be damned if it's going to happen again.

CHAPTER 3

I wake up early on Friday, after a deep dreamless sleep. With the exception of the stint I did traveling in search of my current job, I'm not generally accustomed to waking in an unfamiliar hotel and an unfamiliar town. My assignments as a reporter cover the local beat, and so, for a brief moment, I forget where I am. As I blink my eyes and take in my surroundings, the events of yesterday come flooding back. The unexpected dinner companions, the extraordinary eats and appealing ambiance of the Molly; the vibe of this historic town on the whole somehow makes me feel less a stranger. Actually, I am feeling uncharacteristically comfortable here in Carlisle.

It's barely 6 a.m., but I am anxious to start the day. Hard to believe a man could be so eager to get out of bed and leave the luxurious comforts of this room. But, much as the finer things in life appeal to me, my work is what drives me. It's the reason I get out of bed every single morning, even this bed, with its sheets as smooth as silk and the fluffed up pillows, the likes of which my head has never rested upon and chances are won't again anytime soon after the trial. My enthusiasm to get this day going does not deter me from taking advantage of the one luxury I'd been eyeing since I arrived yesterday. In my hurry to meet Pop Warner for dinner last night, I had put it off. But this morning I allow myself to indulge in the extravagance of the private shower my room offers, a luxury I certainly don't have at home. What an invigorating way to begin a day, letting a stream of warm water rinse off the grime of yesterday's trip without having to wait for a tub to fill. I marvel at the convenience and the way this invention seems to refresh both body and mind simultaneously. A man could easily get used to this, real easily.

After I've showered, shaved, and dressed, I grab my notebook and pencils and head for the lobby. Even though the courthouse is just across the road, I don't plan to return to my room after breakfast. I'm certain that there will be a mob scene, albeit a quiet one, both outside and inside the courthouse so I want to make sure I'm at the hearing room early. I can't think of a better way to continue this morning than with a good cup of Joe in the Molly's dining room, but first, I am in search of a newspaper.

"Good morning, Mr. Murphy," my new friend Jimmy greets me as I approach the front desk. "I hope you had a restful night."

"That I did, Jimmy," I reply. "Full of vim and vigor today, ready to get started."

"Care for a newspaper, sir?"

"You read my mind. Wasn't sure if there'd be one available this early."

"Actually," Jimmy says, "The *Daily Evening Sentinel* printed a special morning edition all about the hearing."

After yesterday's impromptu history lesson, I'm not the least surprised to learn that Jimmy's already read the paper and is more than happy to share his opinions about its contents. I'm beginning to wonder when this guy sleeps. "Ya know, Jimmy, you'd make one heck of a reporter," I say aloud and only half-jokingly. He looks at me quizzically. "You're just right on top of everything, gathering and sharing information; and you really care about what's going on," I explain.

"Is that what it takes to be a reporter?" he asks. "Do you always have to care about what you write about," he asks genuinely, and I am, for a moment, silent.

"I think it certainly helps when you *do* care," I say carefully. "But one of the most important things about being a reporter is to *take care* that what you write is accurate and fair. Once words are in print, they are hard to take back," I sum up, hoping that I've somehow answered

Jimmy's question, though I have barely scratched the surface of what I'd really like to say.

Jimmy nods in agreement and I step down from my invisible soap-box.

"Anyway, there's a lot of good stuff in there," he says as he hands me a copy of the paper. "All sorts of information about the people who'll be testifying, both for and against Mr. Thorpe. If I wasn't working today, I'd be at the courthouse for sure. The King of Sweden's going to be there!"

At this point, Jimmy leans toward me and says quietly, "I'm not supposed to talk about the guests, but King Gustav checked into the hotel last night! Quite a few of the people from the hearing are staying here."

Lord love Jimmy. Although I'm not star struck (except maybe for Pop Warner), I would like to know who's sharing the luxuries of the Molly Pitcher with me. Maybe last night's incredible luck will repeat itself and I'll be able to get some spontaneous interviews. A few direct quotes from the key players will add quite a punch to my story. And it'll be a lot easier to catch them here than at the courthouse, where I'll be one of dozens of reporters firing questions at them.

"Are you having breakfast in the dining room?" Jimmy asks with a sly grin. "I'll bet you'll see a few notable folks in there today."

"Think about what I said, kid," I smile at Jimmy. "If I ever make editor of a paper, I'll hire you in a heartbeat," I say. This is turning into a very interesting morning. I know I can't be the only reporter fortunate enough to be staying here rather than at some flea-bag place on the edge of town, so I think I'd better get into the dining room and start my research.

Thanking Jimmy for the paper and chat, I cross the lobby and enter the dining room, which is occupied by only a handful of people at this early hour. The aroma of coffee fills my nostrils, but there's something else too. It's not the pancakes and bacon, though I can almost taste them. It's something about the air itself. It's like every breath coming from the visitors at the Molly and the residents of Carlisle are simultaneously hanging in mid-air, anticipating the events of this historic hearing.

I ask for a table in the corner, figuring I'll have a good vantage point for watching the "notable folks" enter. Per my usual morning paper routine, I purposefully ignore the headline for the moment and open up to page two, which turns out to be more suitable for my purposes anyway. Here I find articles about the people who will be called to testify, and a quick perusal of the names makes me think that things could get mighty heated in that hearing room today. Since, as Jimmy pointed out, many of them could be eating here in this very room this morning, I decide to entertain myself by playing "Who's Who?" My notepad and pencils always at the ready, my plan is to observe the dining room patrons, jot down anything note-worthy and compare my own annotations with the articles about each witness. From there, I can begin to make educated guesses on the identities of some of the dining room patrons. A guy has to amuse himself, doesn't he?

As the waiter fills my coffee cup and I scan the tables around me , the dining room doesn't seem to contain anyone of interest, so I flip back to look at the headline. "Special Edition! Thorpe Hearing Begins Today," the bold-printed letters proclaim. "An official hearing will begin today at the Cumberland County Courthouse to determine whether famed athlete and local hero Jim Thorpe should be reinstated as an Olympic champion," reads the front-page article. "After astounding the world with gold medal performances in both the pentathlon and decathlon at the 1912 Olympics, Thorpe was accused of having played professional baseball prior to competing in the games in Stockholm. As a result of this allegation, he was stripped of his Olympic medals and titles."

Nothing too earth-shattering here. Just the facts, plain and simple. Or, is that cold and hard? There's a difference.

The first article on page two is, of course, about Jim Thorpe. Lots of background about his childhood and his years at the Indian School, most of which I learned last night from Warner and Friedman. Skimming the article, I pause at the details about Thorpe's current career. Much as I love baseball, I still can't figure out why the greatest athlete of our generation is an outfielder for the New York Giants. I remember when the news first broke a little over two years ago. Thorpe was up for grabs to the professional sports teams since he was obviously no longer an amateur and he made the decision to sign with the Giants. To tell the truth, I didn't think he'd opt for baseball. I thought maybe it left a bad taste in his mouth after what happened. That and, I don't know, something about his unique talent just didn't seem the right fit for that field. So far, I gotta admit, I'm right. Thorpe has shown little of his amazing athletic skills, though from what I read, that hasn't stopped the fans from pouring out to catch a glimpse of the living legend in action. Guess those Giants knew what they were doing.

I'm far more interested in how his next career move will pan out. As a reporter, I already have the inside track that Thorpe will be playing football for the Canton Bulldogs this fall, a field on which, I am willing to bet, he'll shine far more brightly than on that baseball diamond. He is being paid an unfathomable $250 salary to play; I figure he deserves it for the crap he's been through. Besides, I have a feeling, given what he's accomplished so far, that Jim Thorpe will leave his mark on the sport of football in a big way. But that's just me and my big ideas.

I continue reading about the famous, and some infamous and nondescript, individuals who will be giving testimony at Thorpe's hearing. Here it is, King Gustav V of Sweden. Without reading a single word, I am 100-percent certain I can win this round of Who's Who. How hard could it be to pick out royalty? Then again, I am staying at the Molly, I remind myself. Gustav was King when Thorpe won the decathlon and pentathlon at the 1912 Olympics in Stockholm and even presented Thorpe with one of two prizes he received in addition to his medals. It was the first time that "challenge prizes," as the trophies were called, were ever rewarded. As I recall, the IOC demanded that they be returned too, along with the medals.

Reportedly, when the King presented Thorpe with the pentathlon trophy, a bronze bust of the ruler himself, he commented, "You, sir, are the greatest athlete in the world." I'm thinking that the King is a smart guy, but wonder what bearing his observation of Thorpe's talent can have on this hearing. As I scan the dining room, it occurs to me that it's highly unlikely the King will dine among us common folk, even here.

The article goes on to mention that, although the Emperor of Russia, Czar Nicholas, presented Thorpe with the decathlon trophy, which was a jewel-studded chalice in the form of a Viking ship, he won't be at the hearing. I guess one head of state is sufficient as a character witness.

I look up just as the waiter brings my pancakes and eggs and suddenly nearly lose my appetite as I see Charles Clancy, the Carolina coach and source for the story that exposed Thorpe, enter the dining room with another man. Clancy is one of the names on page two of the morning edition. The grumblings of hunger in my stomach are swiftly replaced by something resembling anger stirring inside me as I unwillingly recall my interactions with the man.

It all began when my father and I made our annual pilgrimage to Indiana for a Notre Dame game in November of 1912. Their opponents were the Carlisle Indians, and I can't deny that I was there to root for the Fighting Irish, a fact I wisely chose to keep to myself over coffee with the opposing team's famous coach last night.

Dad had taken two days off from the Slater Mill in Pawtucket, where he worked as a tool-and-dye maker. There were only two things that could make that man take time away from his job—severe illness and Notre Dame's annual game. The fact that Dad hadn't attended Notre Dame was, in his mind, irrelevant.

While I was waiting in line to buy hot chocolate at half-time, a reporter, who'd retired from the *Times* soon after I'd signed on, spotted me. "Bud! How good to see you."

I shook his outstretched hand, scanning my memory for a name. "Here's your coffee, Dan," said a man approaching from the concession stand. Right, Dan Monroe, he'd headed to Eastern Carolina, as I recall, wanting to get away from the New England winters.

"This is a pleasant surprise," I said to Monroe.

"Well, my pal here talked me into making the trip. He just had to see the famous Jim Thorpe play. Bud, meet Charles Clancy, baseball coach for the Winston-Salem team. Charlie, Bud Murphy covers sports for my old paper."

Clancy and I exchanged greetings, and to this day, I wish we'd left it at that. But at Monroe's prodding, Clancy fills me in on the conversation the two had been having throughout the game.

"I've been looking at Thorpe this whole first half," he says carefully, "and damned if I don't finally recognize him. The guy played ball for me in the Carolina League in 1910."

"What do you mean, he played for you?" I asked, my mind working out the dates.

"I mean he played professional ball," Clancy said.

"If I still had a column to write, I'd jump on this story like a cat on a mouse," the seasoned Monroe stated.

So there was my lead for the story of my career. I told Clancy I'd call him the following week and arrange for him to send me any supporting documents he had to back up his claim.

It's not that I didn't believe what the man said, or even that I didn't want to believe it. I just found it incredibly difficult to understand how this had not come to light sooner. It simply wasn't possible that Clancy had missed Thorpe's legendary accomplishments at the Olympic games. And now, almost six months later, he's claming that Thorpe played professional ball for him in Carolina. He'd told me that, although he hadn't recalled the name from his roster, he did recognize Thorpe on the football field. But something just didn't sit right with me. Clancy didn't have enough facts at hand. Did Thorpe earn actual wages? Did he sign a contract? And, if he did play pro, how come no one on the Amateur Athletic Association knew about it? Isn't that their job?

In my opinion, these were all answers a responsible reporter should have before going to print with a story, especially such a potentially explosive story. When I had finally reached him on the office phone, Clancy said he didn't have any of the documentation I wanted handy, but that he would get it. Johnson's story broke the next day, without any of the facts I thought were crucial. I guess there are good reporters and responsible reporters. And here I always thought they were one and the same.

I shake the past from my head, but my gaze is still fixed on Clancy, easily visible in the yet uncrowded dining room. He must feel the glare because he looks at me, then quickly looks at his companion, looks back at me, and goes red in the face.

And then I know I've just won another round of Who's Who. Clancy is having breakfast with Roy Johnson, the reporter who ultimately broke the story. I look back at the newspaper for the short piece about Johnson. Nothing special, just a slapdash reporter who got lucky—with six front page articles and then a promotion to editor. Gee, ain't luck grand?

Well, sour grapes won't do for breakfast so I keep reading, looking for some more appealing characters in the unfolding drama. Here's a little piece about Gus Welch, Thorpe's teammate and close friend.

They attended the Indian School together, and Welch served as best man at Thorpe's wedding two years ago.

By now it's after 8:00, and I gather up my belongings and head for the lobby. I give a quick wave to Jimmy, who is busy attending to another guest, and step out into the bright, hot morning—and stifling, oppressive air. A perfect day for a court hearing.

CHAPTER 4

As I light up my morning cigar, I witness the Town of Carlisle beginning yet another historic day. Residents and shopkeepers are busily preparing for the more-than-usual daily grind, with probably more visitors here for the hearing than this town has seen since maybe the Battle of Carlisle. I am wondering if the current guests in town are as unwelcome as General Stuart and his troops were.

I notice a young man standing nervously across the street from the hotel. He's an Indian who looks to be in his late twenties and he doesn't look happy. Though I imagine today there will be a number of Indians in and around the town, the article I just finished reading described Gus Welch as a full-blooded Chippewa. It also alluded to some bad blood between Welch, the Carlisle Indian School, and some of its former personnel, including my two dinner companions last night. None of this has any real bearing on my story, but it gives me reason to think that this uncomfortable-looking guy across the street just might be Jim Thorpe's former quarterback and best friend. I decide to take a chance.

I cross the street and put out my hand. "Good morning. You in town for the Thorpe hearing?"

The man looks at me uncertainly and nods.

"I'm Bud Murphy, a reporter from Harrisburg. I'm here to cover the hearing."

He finally shakes my hand. "Gus Welch," he says, eyeing me a bit suspiciously.

"No kidding," I say, waving the newspaper in my hand. "I just read here that you're on the list of people being called to testify."

"Yes," he says. "I'll do anything I can to help Jim."

Though I want to, I don't hit him with a barrage of questions. I don't ask whether he knew Thorpe played professional baseball. I don't ask how Thorpe is holding up under all this scrutiny. Instead, I smile and suggest that we head over to the courthouse together.

Welch seems to relax as we begin the short walk to the start of a long, difficult day. Or days. Who knows how long this thing will last? Welch must have read my thoughts, because he wonders the same thing aloud. "How long does something like this take, you think?" he asks me. The guy is smack in the middle of a congressional investigation into the management of the Indian School, and he's asking me how long this might take? I see him glancing around as we walk, and it seems to me that he is perhaps glad for the company. The people of Carlisle, who have always been avid supporters of the Indian School and its students, are probably none too happy with Gus Welch these days.

"I don't know," I reply to his question. "I suppose that depends on how much the witnesses have to say." I hope the comment will create an opening for Welch to begin conversation about Thorpe. I sense there are trust issues here; can't say I blame him and don't want to drive him away.

"I don't know about all the others on that list," Welch begins, "but all I have to say is that Jim Thorpe is a good, honest man who loves to play football." I smile, inside at my ability to generate the discussion, and outwardly at Welch. "The two of you were quite a pair," I comment. Welch had been a football star in his own right, ranked as one of the top three quarterbacks in the nation for Carlisle during those glory days between 1911 and 1913, with a record of thirty-three wins, three losses and two ties.

We reach the courthouse at 8:20 and find a crowd already milling about on the sidewalk. Even at this early hour, I can tell it's going to be another scorcher and decide to head right upstairs to find a seat before the throng ascends.

I can feel the heat increasing as we climb the stairs to the second floor. When we enter the hearing room, I see that all the windows are open, although it doesn't feel much cooler than it did yesterday when they were all shut.

I shake hands with Welch, who moves to the front of the room to find his place among those who will offer testimony. Seeing a handful of people sitting in the jury seats, I realize that this must be where the witnesses will sit, freeing up space in the rows for more spectators.

I choose a seat on the aisle in the next-to-last row. The room's not that big, so I'll be able to see and hear the proceedings without difficulty, and I'll also be able to step out after anyone I think might provide a comment or two without climbing over a row of people.

There are already more than fifty people in the room, most taking seats toward the front. As the room quickly begins to fill, I notice foreign languages and different accents. This really is an international media event. To my right, I hear two men speaking with clipped British accents who are apparently sympathetic to Thorpe. Their notebooks tell me that they are reporters.

"I don't see it," says one of the men. "Simply don't see how a chap with all that talent would risk his name by deliberately breaking a primary rule."

His companion replies, "Too right. I say, Thorpe didn't think the earlier playing had been professional. I think he's being made a scapegoat by this Sullivan bloke."

He is referring to James Sullivan, president of the Amateur Athletic Union and one of the star witnesses against Thorpe. I wish I could understand what the reporters from other countries are saying, whether the majority are pro or con. I have a feeling that much of the European sports press agrees with the British. Too bad for Thorpe that they can't testify.

Looking around the room, I see other men with notebooks on their laps, some of whom I recognize as fellow passengers from yesterday's train ride. I hear accents from across America—flat Midwestern, southern drawl, my own New England. I imagine there's not a paper in the country that won't be covering this event.

At around 9:00, the make-up of the crowd begins to change, and I realize that the locals are beginning to arrive. There are some women entering the room now, but the majority in attendance are men. I recognize a few people from the hotel. The waiter who served my dinner last night is here, wearing street clothes and looking excitedly around the room. I recognize the man with him as one of the bellhops I saw when I checked in yesterday. They take seats in one of the rapidly filling rows, turning toward the back of the room to see who else is entering.

Hearing a bit of commotion at the door, I turn to see a group of teenage boys making their way through.

"Fellas, over here!" a man calls to them from the left aisle.

"Hi, Coach," responds one of the boys. As they file into the room, I overhear a woman in the row behind me say, "That's my Mikey and the high-school baseball team. They all came today to support poor Jim. They just idolize him."

As the team moves toward their coach, taking places standing along the wall of the courtroom, I notice that Mikey's mother didn't speak in the past tense. The boys' devotion to their hero hasn't been diminished by the allegations against him and I jot this down in my notes.

Aside from reporters, whose opinions I don't know, I'd say this room is tilted heavily on the side of "poor Jim." I can't help but wonder what the reaction will be if this hearing doesn't produce the outcome that Carlisle is hoping for.

Within minutes, the folks assembled in the hallway and at the back of the room are abuzz with excitement. Like wedding guests waiting for the bride to make her entrance, everyone turns toward the door.

Glenn Warner is shouldering his way through the crowd right beside Jim Thorpe. Ever the coach, he's shepherding his star player to safety. With his hand firmly grasping Thorpe's elbow, Warner leads the young man up the center aisle to the jury seats, waving off reporters who suddenly leap into action and try to block the aisle.

The media circus has begun.

It's extremely hot in the room, which by now must be crammed with 300 people. They're lining the walls and spilling out into the corridor. Everyone's getting impatient waiting for things to get under way.

At 9:35, the door beside the bench finally opens. A man in his fifties appears and faces the room. He waits a moment for the crowd to notice him and settle down. "All rise. The honorable Edward M. Parker presiding."

The clerk takes his place behind his small desk as the judge enters from the side door and ascends to the bench. He looks to be in his early forties, with dark hair combed severely back from his forehead and dark eyes that hold no glint of humor. To be fair, I sure don't envy him that black robe today.

Judge Parker takes his seat and bangs the gavel once, sharply. He begins immediately.

"This hearing will look into the professional athletic status of James Thorpe—and I will rule as to the status of Mr. Thorpe during the 1912 Olympic Games and the placement of the awards. This is not a trial and there are no lawyers or jury. I will call each witness directly and will review all testimony and evidence. The final decision in this matter will be mine.

"Let me say now that I am aware that emotions in this case run high and that many in this courtroom feel a strong connection to Mr. Thorpe. However, I will not tolerate any outbursts or displays of emotion. This hearing will be conducted in a professional manner and anyone who disrupts the proceedings will be removed from the courtroom for the duration of the hearing."

Well, I guess I can't blame the man for taking a no-nonsense approach. The room is packed, everyone here has a very strong opinion, and it's hot as hell. That combination is bound to lead to disagreements at best, fisticuffs at worst.

The clerk stands. "Will Mr. James Sullivan take the witness stand," he announces.

A murmur runs through the crowd. Although many might expect to see a black-hatted villain, the man who takes the stand more resembles a red-haired leprechaun. I notice that his Irish eyes are not, however, smiling.

Holding a bible in front of Sullivan, the court clerk says, "Raise your right hand. Do you swear to tell the truth, the whole truth, and nothing but the truth, so help you God?"

With his left hand on the bible, Sullivan responds. "I do," he says in a surprisingly deep voice.

"State your name and occupation," says the clerk.

"James Edward Sullivan, President of the Amateur Athletic Union."

At this point the clerk returns to his desk and the judge says, "Mr. Sullivan, briefly tell me the events that led to this hearing."

"Your Honor, during the Olympic Games of 1912, Jim Thorpe won gold medals in both the pentathlon and decathlon events. Following those games, a newspaper article was published, stating that in 1910 Mr. Thorpe had played baseball as a professional, a statement he later corroborated. This is in strict violation of the rules of the International Olympic Committee and the ethical code of the Amateur Athletic Association. For this reason, Mr. Thorpe was stripped of his amateur status and his medals and titles were removed."

Scribbling my notes, I include an observation that Sullivan speaks with a strong certainty, and I can see that this man will not be dissuaded from what appears to be a mission. Thorpe is in for a tough battle.

"Thank you, Mr. Sullivan," says Judge Parker. "You may return to your seat."

The clerk rises and calls for Jim Thorpe to take the stand.

Despite the judge's warning, a spontaneous burst of applause explodes among the spectators as Thorpe stands.

"Order in the court!" demands Parker, rapping the gavel four times for emphasis. "I will not tolerate another such outburst. You will all be banned from this hearing if there is another such display." Like chastened children, the people of Carlisle share victorious little grins as they quiet down.

I watch Thorpe approach the witness stand. I've never seen him this close, and I'm impressed at his size. He's a big man, built for football—and apparently any other sport he sets his mind to as well. His broad face seems almost childlike, and there's an air of naiveté about him that makes him seem likeable. Placing his left hand on the offered bible, Thorpe raises his right hand and promises to tell the truth, the whole truth, and nothing but the truth, so help him God.

The judge speaks. "Mr. Thorpe, will you please read the letter that you sent to Mr. James Sullivan following the accusation that you played professional sports prior to competing in the Olympic Games."

Thorpe reaches into the inside pocket of his jacket and extracts two folded sheets of paper. He looks around nervously, clears his throat, and reads:

Carlisle, Pa.. Jan. 26, 1913.

James E. Sullivan, New York

Dear Sir:

When the interview with Mr. Clancy, stating that I had played baseball on the Winston-Salem team, was shown me, I told Mr. Warner that it was not true and in fact I did not play on that team. But so much has been said in the papers since then that I went to the school authorities this morning and told them just what there was in the stories.

I played baseball at Rocky Mount and at Fayetteville, N.C., in the summer of 1909 and 1910, under my own name. On the same teams I played with several college men from the North who were earning money by ball playing during their vacations, and who were regarded as amateurs at home.

I did not play for the money there was in it, because my property brings me in enough money to live on, but because I liked to play ball. I was not very wise in the ways of the world and did not realize this was wrong and it would make me a professional in track sports, although I learned from the other players that it would be better for me not to let anyone know that I was playing, and for that reason I never told anyone at the school about it until today.

In the fall of 1911, I applied for readmission to this school and came back to continue my studies and take part in the school sports, and of course I wanted to get on the Olympic team and take the trip to Stockholm.

I had Mr. Warner send in my application for registering in the A.A.U. after I had answered the questions and signed it, and I received my card allowing me to compete in the winter meets and other track sports.

I never realized until now what a big mistake I made by keeping it a secret about my ball playing, and I am sorry I did so. I hope I will be partly excused by the fact that I was simply an Indian schoolboy and did not know all about such things.

In fact, I did not know that I was doing wrong because I was doing what I knew several other college men had done, except that they did not use their own names.

I have always liked sport, and only played or run races for the fun of the thing, and never to earn money. I have received offers amounting to thousands of dollars since my victories last summer, but I have turned them all down because I did not care to make money from my athletic skill.

I am very sorry, Mr. Sullivan, to have it all spoiled in this way, and I hope the Amateur Athletic Union and the people will not be too hard in judging me.

Yours truly,
James Thorpe

The judge dismisses Thorpe as soon as he finishes reading the letter, for which Thorpe looks tremendously grateful. To my surprise, he announces that the hearing will conclude for today and will resume on Monday morning.

I look toward the witness seats and see that reporters are pressing in, firing questions at Thorpe. Warner and Welch have formed a protective shield around him, though, and no one is going to get through it. Sullivan is talking with two or three reporters, but most of the press is after the star witness.

I decide to bide my time. Since this is only the first day of the hearing, I figure all the major players will have more to say after a couple days of testimony. And while I don't want to take anything for granted, after hitting it off with Warner last night, I can't help but hope that just maybe he'll introduce me to Thorpe personally.

The spectators are noisily filing out of the courtroom, reacting to both the unexpected delay in the proceedings and Thorpe's letter. Most still sound one-hundred percent behind their local hero and speculate that "there's no way he won't get those medals back." As much as I should remain neutral, I find myself hoping that they're right.

CHAPTER 5

As I prepare to submit my story to the paper the following morning, I read over some of the scratched out copy I don't plan to send to my editor. "A mother in the crowd nods approvingly toward her adolescent son who, along with a group of other impressionable boys, shows up at the hearing not merely to see but to show support for his idol. The locals here have a high regard for their sports and athletes, yes but higher still for honor and pride. An error in judgment is not akin to a purposeful lie. A mistake is not a crime. The punishment does not fit. For the people of Carlisle, these are the unarguable facts."

By the time I am finished editing, I've cut my story to about one-quarter of its original length; the end result is a straightforward, unbiased accounting of the day's events. What I submit to the paper is an informative, though uninspired, piece of journalistic reporting. As it should be, I remind myself.

THORPE READS ALOUD LETTER TO AAU AS HEARING BEGINS

"The people of Carlisle showed up in droves at the Carlisle County Courthouse, many verbal in their support of Jim Thorpe, whose hearing begins today, and hopeful that the medals he was stripped of will be returned. Following a brief statement by James Sullivan, President of the Amateur Athletic Union, Thorpe read aloud the letter he had written to the AAU committee explaining the circumstances leading to the claims that he played professional baseball in Eastern Carolina. Immediately upon the conclusion of Thorpe's read statement, Judge Parker adjourned court for the day. No other witnesses were called to offer testimony. The proceedings will resume on Monday."

What else is there to say, after all? My conversations with Warner and Friedman were colorful and more than I could have hoped for on a personal level. But references to Jim Thorpe were understandably and, I believe purposefully, limited to details about his childhood and glory days of football at the Carlisle Industrial School. We didn't really explore Thorpe's personality, attitude, and work ethic. All I do know of the man is that he is the greatest athlete alive and that he seems like a quiet, reserved guy from his demeanor in the courthouse.

Pop didn't reveal much about his training tactics for Thorpe and the rest of the football team. I can only assume that Warner put Thorpe through a rigorous routine that led him from the training grounds of the Indian School to the most hallowed grounds and revered competition in all of sports, though his Olympic training is another thing we didn't discuss.

As I have a light breakfast in the dining room, I keep thinking about the way Warner and Welch protected Thorpe yesterday. I don't know whether they'd planned it, but those two men swung into action as though their movements had been choreographed. They appeared almost graceful, although their expressions were hard and determined. Once they'd gotten the reporters away from Thorpe, I'd noticed Warner looking my way. Despite the tension in the room, he smiled, maybe in gratitude that I hadn't been part of the advancing herd. He said something to Welch and Thorpe, who both looked in my direction, and then he and Gus talked for a few moments.

I also keep trying to picture Thorpe at the Indian School and wonder what it was about the place that made him decide to return there. He had left for awhile to work on a farm but went back to the school three years later. Since today is Saturday, and I have nothing pressing planned, maybe I'll pay a visit to the Indian School to get a feel for the place and see if I can't find some more background for my story.

The desk clerk calls my name as I cross the lobby. Ah, I guess Jimmy does get some time off, after all. The young man hands me a note.

"Mr. Murphy," I read. "I would like the opportunity to talk more with you about Jim Thorpe. I will arrive at the hotel at 10:00 AM and hope that you are willing to see me."

It's signed by Gus Welch.

A glance at the grandfather clock at the foot of the stairs tells me that it's 9:40. I suppose another cup of coffee won't hurt while I wait for Welch to arrive.

He walks through the front door at ten sharp looking less nervous than he did yesterday as he scans the lobby.

"Good morning, Gus," I say as we shake hands. "I was pleased to get your note."

"I thought maybe I can tell you some things about Jim. We've been close buddies for years, since we first went to the Indian school, and I suppose I know him as well as anyone."

"Funny you should mention the school," I say. "I was thinking about it, wondering if it might be a good idea to visit out there and see the place for myself."

Gus's eyes brighten at the thought. "I'd say that's a real good idea, Mr. Murphy. If you'd like, I'll go with you so I can fill you in on the time Jim spent there. In fact, the school's where Jim and Iva are staying while they're in town."

Okay, this is just about too good to be true. Jim Thorpe is staying at the Carlisle Indian School, which I'm about to visit with his best friend. Today might be the day I get the interview that every reporter in town would kill for.

It's another sweltering morning as we leave the hotel and turn off Main Street onto a narrow lane. "This is the road we walked back to school whenever we came into town," explains Welch. "We followed these old trolley tracks, running around the trees, playing tag along the way to pass the time."

It's actually a nice walk, despite the heat. As we approach a small footbridge, Welch begins to reminisce about ice skating on the surrounding ponds. "After a good freeze, us boys would dam up the creek. The banks on both sides would flood and we'd have a perfect spot for skating."

I ask if Thorpe skated along with the others.

"Sure did," says Gus. "And I guess it's no surprise that he was about the best skater of us all. Sometimes we'd play hockey, and sure enough, whichever team Jim was on usually won."

He gives a soft chuckle. "A bit farther north there's a natural pond that freezes over on its own, but the ice there was never as good as what we had here. But our hockey games were so good that folks from town would come to watch us play and the white kids never touched this ice if we were around. They always let us have it for a game."

We continue walking as Welch tells this story, and despite the cool imagery he's conjuring, I find myself rolling up my shirtsleeves against the heat. It takes about forty minutes to reach the school.

As we approach the gate, I ask Welch what the day-to-day life of students was like. He explains that the school day was divided into two sessions, one for academics and the other for trades. Reading, writing, and arithmetic were taught in the academic sessions. During trade classes, the boys learned carpentry, tinsmithing and blacksmithing; the girls were taught cooking, sewing, laundry, and other domestic skills.

"Captain Pratt really believed strongly in his military training, so that's the way he ran the school," Welch says. "The boys wore uniforms and the girls wore old-fashioned dresses. We had to march to classes and ate all our meals in the dining hall. We were split up into companies and some students were officers. There was drill practice and a military-style court system. It was very strict."

Listening to him, I can almost see why Thorpe ran away. Coming from a fairly unstructured life to what amounts to a military school must have been incredibly hard for those kids. I wonder how often the military tribunal was used to determine punishment, since I'll bet there was a lot of rebellion.

"Were the teachers any good?" I ask, "or was it more about discipline than education?"

"Actually, our school had an excellent newspaper and magazine." The answer surprises me. "We had some very good writers in our class. And we had debating societies where we discussed politics and other issues. It was the debates that made me interested in going to law school."

I try to pull a poker face, but I think Welch sees my reaction. He smiles proudly. "Yep, I'm planning to graduate from Dickinson Law in the class of '17. Don't know yet what I'll do afterward, though."

"Maybe you'll follow in Pop's footsteps," I say, "and combine your legal and football skills."

This comment elicits no response, and I wonder whether there are hard feelings between Welch and Warner because of the congressional hearing. Even if there are, at least they're united in helping Thorpe through this hearing.

Welch points out the various buildings—administration offices, mess hall, and the guardhouse, where students found guilty of serious offenses were put in isolation as punishment. When we reach the dorms, he points to a low building to the right.

"That's where we lived, Jim and me," he says. "Wasn't too bad. Pretty comfortable once we got used to it." But I notice that there's little expression in his voice now. Again, I think of how difficult it must have been for young people to be brought here and forced to live a life completely different from anything they'd known.

Across the road, a woman stands in front of a building identical to the one Welch has pointed out. "Girls' dorm," he says, but this time he smiles. "And there's Iva."

As we cross the road, I'm struck by the woman's appearance. She's quite young, seems to be barely twenty, and fairly tall, with beautiful dark eyes and hair. And a lovely smile. She and Gus greet one another warmly and he makes the introductions.

"Iva, this is Mr. Bud Murphy, a reporter who's covering Jim's hearing. Mr. Murphy, this is Iva Thorpe."

"I'm pleased to meet you, Mrs. Thorpe. Gus has been telling me about your husband and about what it was like living here at the school."

"It's nice to meet you too, Mr. Murphy. I'm glad Gus has been able to help you to get to know Jim."

She suggests that we walk to the mess hall where we can mercifully find a cool drink. Gus and I take seats on a porch of the dining hall, while Iva goes inside to look for beverages. She returns in a few minutes carrying a tray with a pitcher of lemonade and three tall glasses. She sits down and pours each of us a welcome glass of the ice-cold drink.

Not wanting to sound too much like a reporter going for the kill, I decide to hold off on questions about Thorpe and instead ask Iva about her experience at the school.

"Oh, it's probably not much different from anything Gus told you," she says. "Except of course that the girls learned to cook and sew and run a home instead of the hard skills the boys were taught."

When I ask if there was anything in particular that she disliked about the school, she nods. "Yes, there were a few things," she says firmly. "It was very hard to get used to dressing like a white girl. The shoes hurt my feet and the dresses felt so tight. It was hard to be comfortable. And it felt very strange for us to be taught together with boys. I was always embarrassed to have to stand and recite a lesson or a poem, because we had never been taught that way at home. I preferred to write my lessons instead of speaking in the classroom."

I ask if students were allowed to return to their families during school breaks.

"We would be sent to families in town for the summer," Iva responds. "We had to work for them, on their farms or in their homes. Some were nice, but others were not."

Welch nods. "Most of us hated it," he says. "We all missed our families, but Captain Pratt thought that if we went home, we either wouldn't come back or we'd fall back on old ways."

"But we never got the chance to prove him wrong," Iva says sadly.

"Did Jim have any difficulty adjusting to living at the school?" I ask.

Iva and Gus exchange a smile. "You could say that," Thorpe's wife replies. "Jim first came to the school in 1904, but dropped out later that year after his father died. He worked on a farm for about three years before he came back here. He'd played some sports before he ran away and I really think that's what made him come back, the chance to play again."

Iva goes on to tell me that Thorpe returned to Carlisle in 1907 at age nineteen. She arrived at the school in 1909, when she was sixteen. Welch begins to laugh.

"I used to like to rib Jim, because he noticed Iva right away but was too shy to talk to her. He kept waiting for a chance to 'accidentally' get to speak to her. Remember, Iva?"

"Yes, I do," she smiles. "I was even more shy than Jim; I'm surprised we ever talked to each other at all, let alone got married."

When I ask about the wedding, she says brightly, "Oh, it was lovely. We were married at Saint Patrick Church. Father Stock, the Indian School chaplain, and Father Welsh at St. Patrick's Church both said the Mass. Gus was the best man. Jim looked so handsome. It was a perfect day, even more so because we were able to have a mass for our wedding."

"I'm sure you were a beautiful bride," I say. Now it's time to get to the point. "What's happened to your husband, since the Olympics must be difficult for you?"

"It is," she answers quickly, "because I hate to see how it upsets Jim. He never knew he was doing anything wrong and he's the most upset to think that people believe he lied. That's the worst part."

Then she dashes my hopes for an exclusive with Thorpe when she says, "I so wish Jim was here today to talk with you. You seem different from the other reporters who push and push him for answers. I think he'd like to tell you his side. But he's off with Mr. Warner, talking about the hearing and what he'll do next season."

I stress that I'd be very pleased to have the opportunity to talk with Thorpe personally, hoping that she might still be able to make it happen. At this point, there's not much more to say, so Welch and I take our leave and start the hot walk back to town.

The rest of the day is spent working on my story, writing up some background about the school and Thorpe's life there. After a simple meal, I decide to take advantage of that relaxing shower again after walking to the school and back in the heat. I consider having a brandy and a cigar, but opt for turning in early.

I wake well rested on Sunday, none too sorry that I skipped the brandy the night before. I dress in a light suit and leave the hotel at 6:45 to walk around the corner to St. Patrick's Church on East Pomfret Street. It's not yet too hot and the church is dark and cool. Mass begins promptly at 7:00, and I listen closely to the priest's sermon about the painful repercussions of bearing false witness. "Thorpe fan," I think.

When the service ends, I follow the priest up the aisle, where he stands on the top step of the church to greet parishioners.

I wait for the regulars to speak with him before I approach. "I enjoyed your sermon, Father," I say. "It seems most appropriate in light of what's going on in town this week."

"Are you visiting us for the hearing?" he asks.

"Yes, sir. I'm writing about it for the *Evening News*. My name is Bud Murphy."

The priest extends his hand and smiles. "Father Welsh. Pleased to have you in our congregation this morning."

"I heard your name yesterday," I reply. "I had the opportunity to speak with Mrs. Thorpe and she told me about her wedding."

"Oh yes. Iva is a lovely young woman. Her faith is remarkable. I think it's helping her quite a lot during this difficult time."

His remark reminds me of something that Iva Thorpe said yesterday. "Father, she made a point of stressing how important it was that the wedding ceremony was a mass. In retrospect, it almost seems as if she thought there'd be an objection to it. Was someone at the school against the marriage?"

"That's not it at all," Father Welsh replies. He glances at his watch. "If you're interested in the background, why not join me in the rectory for breakfast? The next mass isn't until nine, and it would be nice to have some company."

I eagerly accept, amazed at how many times since I've hit town people have just invited me to talk with them. When we enter the rectory, we're greeted by a middle-aged Indian woman. Father Welsh addresses her as Martha and asks her to serve breakfast for two.

As we take seats in the cozy dining room, Martha quickly sets a second place at the table. She exits the room, returning barely a minute later with coffee and a basket of freshly baked muffins.

Father Welsh looks to be in his late sixties, with thinning gray hair and soft blue eyes. "I've only been in this parish for five years," he says. "But my predecessor was here for many years and a good number of them were spent butting heads with Pratt."

The priest explains that Pratt insisted his Indian students attend religious services in the chapel every Sunday and sometimes during the week as well. A staunch Protestant with little or no tolerance for the Catholic Church, he refused to allow students who had been baptized Catholic on their reservations to attend mass at St. Patrick's.

"That seems unnecessarily intolerant," I observe.

"I agree," says Father Welsh. "But like so many issues, money and politics were at the root of the problem. You see, despite the separation of church and state, the government was willing to fund religious missions as a way of assimilating the Indians into our culture. Needless to say, every denomination wanted some of the money."

By now Martha has brought two plates heaped with scrambled eggs and side dishes of bacon and warm toast. Father Welsh continues as we begin to eat.

"Unfortunately, there was a good deal of anti-Catholic sentiment a hundred or so years ago, and when the Federal Indian Office began establishing schools on the reservations, the Church didn't carry much weight. In the 1870s the government set up contract schools that were run by missionaries and received funds based on the number of students in attendance."

I'm trying to figure out how Pratt's anti-Catholicism figures into this story but don't want to interrupt. I can tell that the man is anxious to share all of his information and I'm enjoying the excellent coffee while I listen.

"The Bureau of Catholic Indian Missions was formed to help Catholics reach more Indians in the western territories."

He pauses to spread jam on a piece of toast and eats half the slice before continuing. "Now here's where Pratt enters the picture," he says, before taking a sip of coffee. "Pratt wouldn't allow his students to attend mass, so the Catholic contract schools stopped sending him pupils. And once he realized that he couldn't get any new pupils, he refused to allow Catholic students to practice their religion at the school. It was a vicious cycle of unfairness, but he refused to alter his position."

"Since he was an administrator, I'm surprised that he'd let his dislike of Catholicism control his decisions. He must have really hated us." I laugh.

"It's true," says the priest. "Once the authorities realized that Pratt was forcing Catholic students to worship in Protestant churches, the director of the Bureau of Catholic Indian Missions got involved. He asked Father Ganss, my predecessor, to do something about the situation."

"That must have been a mighty tall order," I say. "It sounds as though it would've taken the cavalry to move Pratt on the issue."

Father Walsh laughs. "Good choice of words," he says. "Because organizing the troops is pretty much what Father Ganss did. When he realized that he couldn't fight Pratt alone, he contacted Sister Katharine Drexel in Philadelphia, asking for money to fund a school for the Catholic Indian students here in Carlisle. She was a champion of funding schools for these kids.

"Well, to make a long story short," he continues, and I smile inwardly at yet another spontaneous history lesson from a Carlisle resident, "Ganss finally contacted the Catholic Missions Bureau about the discrimination, forcing Pratt to correct the situation."

In the long run, Pratt eventually saw the benefit of working with the Catholic Church, rather than against it. Ultimately Carlisle became the model for cooperation between government schools and churches and, under the "Carlisle Plan," Pratt not only permitted his students to attend mass at St. Patrick's, he also allowed missionaries to visit the school and offer religious instruction. In light of this progress, Sister Drexel donated the enormous sum of $8000 to the parish, which was used to build a school for the Catholic Indians and negroes in Carlisle. The school was completed in 1901 and dedicated as St. Katharine's Hall.

After Pratt left the school in 1904, his successors, including Moses Friedman, maintained a cooperative relationship with Father Ganss and St. Patrick's.

Father Welsh and I finish our breakfast and talk for another few minutes about Thorpe and the hearing. As Thorpe's priest, he likes the athlete and is solidly in his corner, a fact that doesn't surprise me.

Taking my leave of the rectory, I thank Father warmly for his hospitality, and express my appreciation for the kindness I've been shown since I arrived in Carlisle. Walking back to the hotel, I decide to spend the afternoon leisurely reading the newspaper on the hotel porch. Maybe with that cigar I skipped last night.

CHAPTER 6

As I rise and shine and ready myself for the much-anticipated start of the Jim Thorpe hearing—the true reason for my being here—I realize how very much at home I feel in Carlisle. I came here to report on the outcome of a single event; the stakes are significant to be sure, in terms of one man's reputation and in terms of the integrity of amateur sports. Yet, over the course of the past four days, I've learned more about sport, American history, Indians, honor, and pride than any classroom could ever teach. I am comfortable in my hotel room, in the streets, and most surprisingly, with the people of this remarkable town.

They are welcoming and gracious, despite the fact that most of the out-of-towners are here to report on something they view as negative and unfair. Although I've eaten several meals by myself while in town, this isn't so unusual for me even back in Providence. I've managed to make a few acquaintances, one of whom I have admired for quite some time. And, as much as I would sure like to make the acquaintance of Carlisle's most famous resident, whom I have idolized for years, I'm sure Jim Thorpe has plenty to occupy his time and his mind right now. "Who knows what this day will have in store, though," I say aloud to myself, because I have almost come to expect to meet someone interesting and discover something new around every corner in this town.

I have no real interest in breakfast today, but I like when the waiter asks if I'll be having the usual as I sit at my regular table in the dining room. "Best pancakes I've ever had, Tim; sure, why not?" I reply. As I glance at the morning paper, I'm glad I ordered breakfast. Looks to be a long, busy day in the courthouse, with the Amateur Athletic Union, the United States Olympic Committee, and the International Olympic Committee all making presentations. I don't want my stomach grumbling in the middle of the proceedings, not that anyone would hear it amidst all the other grumbling that's sure to come from the spectators who will likely be less than thrilled with what these organizations have to say.

I don't recognize any of the dining room patrons as participants in the hearing, so I concentrate my attention on the news.

I see that Pop Warner is scheduled for a presentation to the court, as well as Richard Henry Pratt. The background information in the article isn't nearly as complete as the details I have gathered over the last few days. Reading about history is one thing. Talking to people who have made or experienced history is quite another. I'm anxious to see Pop Warner take the stand and curious to observe Pratt, the man who conceived the idea for the Carlisle Indian School. After yesterday's lesson from Father Welsh, I know there are some less than admirable qualities about Pratt, though I'm sure he views his initial intentions as purely honorable. I feel the need to get to that courthouse pronto and don't even finish off my pancakes, though I do drain the last mouthful of coffee in my cup.

I arrive at the courthouse two minutes later, not having consciously observed a single person or thing. Very unlike me. I'm always worried I'll miss the next big story if I'm not paying attention. But the big story is right here, unfolding all around me, and I'd like to think that I have a better handle on it than any of these other media hounds.

Slightly distracted and trying to refocus my reporter instincts, I manage to not see the gentleman standing directly in front of me, who I almost knock to the ground. "Whoa, sorry there, pal," I say apologetically. "Didn't see you there." How I could have missed him is beyond me. He's very well-dressed, in a much more obvious way than anyone else here. I figure him to be a foreigner and guess I'm right when I can't quite understand what he's saying to me. It sounds like "God morgon," and I realize it is a greeting.

"Good morning to you," I reply. "Not from around here, are you?" His name, I learn, is Fredrik, and it seems he is here to report on today's proceedings too. Not for a newspaper, though, but for his employer, none other than King Gustav V of Sweden. The wheels in my head are already turning. "I'd heard the King was in town," I answer knowingly. "I think we may even be staying in the same hotel."

Fredrik informs me that the King has been asked to offer his testimony the next day, and has assigned him to give an accounting of the day's events. No one would expect the King to unnecessarily sit through a day of lengthy testimony in a hot, crowded public building, though apparently it was very important to His Majesty that he attend Jim Thorpe's hearing in person. "That's an awfully long way to travel," I state the obvious. "Why is it so important to him?" Fredrik says that the King took great pride in hosting the Games of the V Olympiad, and is also a great admirer of athletes and sports. Not many people know that he is an avid tennis player and often plays under the name Mr. G so as not to attract attention.

"Who'd have thought I have something in common with a king," I respond. "I've played tennis for years."

I'm still curious if Gustav is here to ensure that Sweden is above reproach in its conduct during the games or if he is here as a supporter of Thorpe. His comments to Thorpe when presenting the medals and awards were well noted in the press. But there's no time for more questions, as Fredrik and I go our separate ways. Me to the section in the courtroom reserved for reporters, him to the area reserved for witnesses. Today, in the absence of the King, he gets the royal treatment.

Judge Parker enters the courtroom and calls the room to order. An immediate silence falls over the spectators. After the weekend, everyone is looking forward to moving the proceedings along. He announces that the AAU, USOC, and IOC will each be asked to detail the reasons why Jim Thorpe was disqualified from the 1912 Olympic Games.

First up is the AAU. James Sullivan once again takes the stand and is reminded by the court clerk that he is still under oath. "Mr, Sullivan," Judge Parker begins. "You stated on Friday that Mr. Thorpe played professional ball and that, in your words, "this is in strict violation of the rules of the International Olympic Committee and the ethical code of the Amateur Athletic Association."

"Yes, your honor. That is correct." Sullivan replies.

"How long has the AAU been in existence, Mr. Sullivan?"

"The organization was founded in 1888. About twenty-seven years ago," says Sullivan.

"How long have you been associated with the AAU?"

"Actually, I was one of the founding members."

"I see," Parker says, leaning back in his chair. "And, as one of the founders, you would be most familiar with the organization's guidelines and standard practices, or as you stated, its ethical code?"

"Of course I am," Sullivan says.

Parker almost, but doesn't quite, glare at him. "A simple "yes, your honor" will suffice Mr. Sullivan."

"Yes, your honor," Sullivan repeats and there is muffled laughter in the courtroom. Before the judge can even grab his gavel, the court goes quiet.

"And, precisely what is the purpose of the AAU?" asks Parker.

"Well, our purpose is to promote the development of amateur sports and support and advance the growth of the amateur athlete."

"Define amateur, please."

"In terms of an athlete, an amateur is someone who has never played professionally or received monetary compensation for his play."

"Would you say there is room for interpretation in this rule, Mr. Sullivan?"

"No, your honor, I would not."

"I see," says the judge, though it doesn't appear to me that Parker sees this at all. He makes a note of some sort and rests his eyes on a document on top of one of the piles on his desk.

"Mr. Sullivan, does the AAU screen its members?" he asks.

"Screen, your honor?" Sullivan asks hesitantly.

I am smiling as I look at the very same question in my own notes. Damn, I'm good. Maybe I should have considered the law route. I look over at where Jim Thorpe is seated, and a flash of a smile, or something close, briefly crosses his face. Sullivan seems to have flinched at the question and Thorpe must have felt a twinge of satisfaction at seeing his adversary on the hot seat.

"Does the AAU check the backgrounds of its potential members to ensure that they are eligible? Why was the AAU unaware for years, according to my notes, that Mr. Thorpe had played professional ball?" Parker inquires.

Sullivan stammers something about procedures and that it is impossible to track the background of every individual in the organization. "A man's word should stand on its own merit," he declares, and the courtroom erupts at the obvious insult.

As the crowd jeers and the judge bangs his gavel, I look again at Thorpe, his eyes fixed and narrow, his jaw firm, but his head still high. *He is an honorable man and really didn't know that he did anything wrong*, I think to myself. And, for the very first time since I lost the damned story, I know, without doubt or regret, that I did the right thing. Case closed. For me, though unfortunately, not for Thorpe.

"Mr. Sullivan, I will ask you to refrain from comments or conjecture other than direct response to my questions. Do I make myself clear?" Parker proclaims, as he lays down his gavel and continues. "So, the AAU gave Mr. Thorpe amateur status, is that correct?"

"Yes."

"And, that status has since been revoked?"

"Yes. We learned that Mr. Thorpe had played professional baseball for an Eastern Carolina league in 1909–1910, a good two years prior to his appearance in the 1912 Olympics."

"Through a newspaper reporter, is that correct?"

"Yes, initially. However, Mr. Thorpe himself admitted to it. He read the letter right here in this courtroom, admitting that he participated in the Olympics after he played professional ball."

"I want to be clear on this, Mr. Sullivan. Are you saying that Mr. Thorpe himself admitted to participating in an amateur competition knowing full well that he was a professional?" Parker asks.

"Yes, your honor, that is what I am saying," Sullivan answers.

I'm a bit confused at the judge's belaboring of this point, when he holds up what is apparently Jim Thorpe's letter to the AAU.

"I don't see anything in here that says exactly that."

"Well, not exactly," Sullivan admits. The courtroom spectators murmur and I acknowledge to myself that I'm much better at reporting than I would have been at law.

"What exactly did Mr. Thorpe admit to, Mr. Sullivan?" Parker already seems on the verge of losing patience, and Sullivan is only the first witness of the day. I feel sorry for the others.

"He admitted that he played for Rocky Mountain in Fayetteville in the Class D, Eastern Carolina League in 1909–1910."

"Thank you. I have the rest of the details right here. Let's move on. What was the AAU's course of action after this revelation?"

"We held a vote and decided to retroactively withdraw Mr. Thorpe's amateur status," Sullivan holds up a sheet of paper. "May I read from this, as to be accurate, your Honor?"

Parker nods.

"The decision of the AAU is to secure the return of prizes and re-adjustment of points won by him [Thorpe], and to immediately eliminate his records from the books," Sullivan reads.

"Thank you. That will be all, Mr. Sullivan," Parker dismisses him.

I'd done a bit of my own research on Sullivan, so it's no surprise to me that even after all of the grilling, he walks away a cool and confident man. He's fairly influential in the world of amateur sports, had a successful career in sports publishing, and even served on the New York Board of Education. The guy is no slouch. Poor Thorpe was certainly no match for him and the rest of the vultures that began to circle after that news story broke. Maybe this hearing is a good thing after all.

Representatives from the United States Olympic Committee and the International Olympic Committee are similarly questioned by Judge Parker. Nothing that everyone doesn't already know is revealed by either organization. By now, I can recite from memory Rule 26 of the Olympic Charter, which has been referred to or read aloud multiple times, reiterating the strict rules regarding amateur status for athletes participating in the Olympics. Essentially, the rule states that athletes who received money prizes for competitions, who were sports teachers, or who had previously competed against professionals, were not considered amateurs, and were not allowed to compete in the Olympic games. I briefly speculate as to the wisdom behind this rule, but who am I to question it?

Judge Parker announces that he will call one final witness to make a presentation to the court before recessing for lunch. When Glenn Warner takes the stand, he appears nervous, pale, and quite unlike the self-assured coach and dinner companion I knew. It's difficult to figure this out, as I would think Warner confident enough to hold his own on any field. He was, after all, a law school graduate who must have been relatively comfortable in this environment. But, then again, he has a personal stake in these proceedings. He is Thorpe's mentor. Thorpe was as much under his guidance and supervision while at the Indian School as anyone's. And, obviously, Thorpe meant a great deal to Warner, not just as a football player, but as a young man. So, for these reasons, I think I understand Warner's reticence. While listening to his testimony, I slowly begin to realize how wrong I am.

"Mr. Warner," Judge Bidell begins, "I would like to hear details about your interactions with Jim Thorpe while at the Carlisle Indian School. However, before we get to that, I think I may have misplaced some of the paperwork regarding this case. Do you have a copy of your correspondences with the AAU or IOC regarding the reinstatement of Mr. Thorpe's medals?"

Warner shifts uncomfortably in his seat, averting his eyes and looking almost awkward and chagrined. "No, your honor," he replies, "I do not." Before the judge can put another question to him, Warner continues. "I never wrote any letters on behalf of Mr. Thorpe."

An astonished murmur rises among the spectators. The quizzical expression on Judge Bidell's face while questioning Warner is replaced with annoyance as he reaches for his gavel. "Order," he bellows, pounding the tool of his trade fiercely on the mahogany. "This courtroom will come to order or I will have the lot of you removed."

It's obvious that no one wants to get thrown out of these proceedings, and the crowd becomes as silent as falling snowflakes. Now, that would be a welcome sight, I can't help but think, as I adjust my tie, loosening it just a tad to let some air in under my collar. Pop Warner must have felt hot under the collar too, but the judge merely responds, "I see," and moves on with his intended line of questioning. Warner interrupts before the judge can even begin. "I did help Jim compose that letter he wrote to Mr. Sullivan," Pop quickly interjects.

"We'll get to that all in good time, Mr. Warner," Judge Parker replies. "I simply wanted to ensure that all copies of correspondences and documents with pertinent information were in my possession," he says sternly.

"Of course, Your Honor," Warner replies, with a renewed sense of confidence and composure.

Judge Parker sits back in his chair, which looks a lot more comfortable than the unforgiving wood benches the rest of us are seated on. He asks Pop Warner to give some background about Jim Thorpe and how he came to attend the Carlisle Indian School. I glance around the courtroom after the judge poses this question. Though there isn't a man, woman, or child present who doesn't know the story; every spectator's eyes are fixed intently on Warner, their ears hanging on his every word.

Warner recounts much of the information he told me over dinner at the Molly. While he is speaking, I am unable to take my eyes off Thorpe, thinking again, as I did four nights ago, how difficult life must have been for him and all of those Indian boys. He doesn't strike me, however, as a man who wants anyone's sympathy.

"How did you come to make Mr. Thorpe's acquaintance at the school," Parker is asking.

"I was fortunate enough to be Carlisle's football coach at the time. I had worked there a few years earlier, but left for a coaching position at another school. Jim left the school, too, after his father died, and then came back. I guess we were destined." Pop grins. "I was always looking for guys who had some talent or showed potential. There was something about Jim, you could just tell. Not that he's a big guy or anything. Heck, he's not even six-feet tall, but he had all the right stuff in all the right places. And he could run like the wind," Pop beams while he's talking. "We were all shocked at this amazing athlete in our midst, and of course, excited about him, too."

"Was Mr. Thorpe considered a good student while attending the Indian School?" asks Parker.

"I would say so, yes," answers Warner. "Like all those boys, he had his problems. Had to make a lot of adjustments. But, overall, he was better than most grades wise, and the best of the best athletic wise," Warner adds.

"I am referring specifically to grades and behavior, Mr. Warner."

"As far as I recall, he received all 'good' and 'very good' marks on his record at the school. As for his behavior, I had to discipline him a time or two, but nothing out of the ordinary. He was—is—a good young man."

When Parker asks what Thorpe did to elicit disciplinary action, every spectator in the courtroom is leaning forward in their seats. "The only clear incident I can recall, Your Honor, was when Jim ended up drunk after a game one night. I had to come and pick him up. I wouldn't let him play until he apologized to his teammates and promised not to drink again," Warner states.

"Did he?" Judge Parker asks, seeming more curious than judge-like.

"Yes, he did." Warner replies simply.

Judge Parker jots down a few more notes and then asks Warner if he considers himself more than a coach to Thorpe. Warner seems taken aback by the question, but gathers himself before he responds.

"In the beginning, my role in Jim's life was clearly as a coach. I had in my possession, if you will, a gifted, promising, natural athlete with skills and ability beyond a coach's wildest dreams. In me, Jim had an exceptional and experienced coach, who could take him to feats beyond *his* wildest dreams. We were a great team. As time went on, I saw beyond the boy's athletic needs and became a father-figure to him, or at least I would like to think so. As more time has passed and the boy has grown, marrying the lovely Iva, and becoming a man in his own right, facing and rising to not only the greatest athletic challenge of all time, but this, the greatest challenge of his life, I am proud to consider myself Jim Thorpe's friend."

Warner is an eloquent a speaker and that is as good a closing argument as I have ever heard. Too bad the hearing's only just begun. He really could have been a lawyer. The courtroom erupts into applause, which does not go over well with the judge, who bangs his gavel in aggravation and recesses the court for lunch.

Hurrying to the Hamilton Restaurant, which is a scant one block away and which my buddy Jimmy tells me has good eats and quick service, I catch a glimpse of Fredrik ambling out of the courthouse. I invite him to join me for a hot dog and laugh aloud when he inquires as to what that might be. The Hamilton is in a prime location, right next to the train station on West High Street, but since the hearing went so long this morning, the afternoon lunch crowd is long gone. Fredrik and I enjoy a quick meal, sharing stories of our lives and thoughts about Carlisle, Jim Thorpe, and the hearing. When I ask him if he was present at the Olympic Games, he nods eagerly while taking a bite of his hot dog, which he appears to be enjoying as much as any delicacy. As he describes watching Thorpe perform, I tell him that I envy him. He looks at me strangely and neither of us comments further on my ridiculous remark.

When we return to the courthouse, we find that Colonel Richard Henry Pratt is set to make his presentation. He too reveals much of the historical information I have already been made privy to. You could tell the man bore a grudge against the system that ultimately took away his project—the Carlisle Indian School. He reflects briefly on the early days and his intentions when beginning the program. Judge Parker requests details about the time Thorpe attended the school. "He was a fairly typical Indian boy," Pratt remarks, "his first time around. He left the program in 1904, less than a year after he arrived. We marked his record as a "deserter." I have no real memories of him during that time. Which is to say, he did nothing remarkable or negligible to impact the school," the colonel comments.

"And, upon his return?" Parker prods. Pratt remarks that by the time Thorpe returned to the school, the football program had flourished, indicating how successful his ideologies and practices had been for the school, the students, and the town of Carlisle. The judge tolerates the self-indulgence for about a minute and then asks again about Thorpe. "While Mr. Thorpe was at Carlisle from 1907–1912, under the extraordinary guidance of its teaching and coaching staff, he attained great personal success for himself as a man and great accolades for the Indian School as a sound and successful institution of learning," Pratt concludes. I find myself unable to like or dislike this man. His initial purpose may have been to "kill the Indian to save the man," but without his misguided intention, who knows what would have become of Jim Thorpe and so many others?

Mercifully, the judge dismisses court for the day, though not that much of the day remains. I return to the Molly, or home as I now think of it, and find that I am exhausted. Not physically as much as mentally. So many circumstances, so many views, so many opinions, to ponder and weigh. And—I almost forgot—to report about! Looks like room service again.

CHAPTER 7

Back in the courthouse on Tuesday, I have to remind myself what day it is. It feels like I've just left here which, of course, I pretty much have. This morning, I spent some time talking with Jimmy at the front desk. This time, it's me filling him in on what's going on at the hottest event in town, maybe the world. He is almost seething when I tell him about James Sullivan's presentation on the stand and questions aloud how a guy like that could be in charge of an organization as good as the AAU.

"It's a business, Jimmy, my friend. Just like any other," I reply with all my worldly wisdom.

Jimmy shrugs. "I remember when there was a problem here at the Molly and one of the guests blamed me outright for a mistake I didn't make. The management here stood up for me," he declares proudly. "You'd think that the AAU would at least stand by its members, especially someone as great as Jim Thorpe, instead of hangin' 'em out to dry," he adds. Yeah, you would think.

Instead, though, here they are creating a scene of epic proportion on a worldwide stage, with an international audience that is quite possibly wondering what the heck is wrong with these foolish Americans. The AAU doesn't know what's going on in its own organization? It doesn't support its athletes? America cheats? This entire incident is a lose-lose situation. I am pulling for one person to come out a winner, though. To hell with impartiality. If I had a vote, I'd give Thorpe back his medals, and I'm willing to bet that most of the country and the rest of the world would do the same.

Waiting around for the trial to begin, I actually find myself talking to people I have no real desire to speak with. Other reporters, voicing their opinions, spurting out the facts as they know them, boasting about an interview with a local shopkeeper who knew Thorpe back in his Carlisle football days. I smile to myself. What these guys would give to have met the people I have and had the conversations that I did. True to my nature, I keep it all to myself. I thought that trait was a curse when I lost the big story. Now I know better. I would hate myself if I were the guy who caused this whole mess in the first place.

I settle into my usual seat with plenty of time to spare before the hearing begins. I want to review the local news, since talking with Jimmy didn't leave me much time to do so this morning. Not that I minded. It was my initial conversation with him my first day in town that set off a chain of chance meetings and events that have served me quite well, professionally and personally. Some of his perspective has subtly influenced my own point of view and some has even found its way into my articles, a fact that my editor did not hesitate to point out. But, as I recall, he didn't dwell on it, either.

The local news details the day's court presentations. I'm beginning to think I don't really need to even be present at the hearing these days, since most of the witnesses are people I've already met and spoken to at great length: Gus Welch, Pop Warner, Moses Friedman, King Gustav V. Alright, I haven't actually met the King, but I did introduce one of his attendants to that fine American delicacy, the hot dog. And I did learn a good deal from Fredrik, which is about as close as I am going to get to a personal interview with the King. Let's be serious here, Murphy, I tell myself as I place an "X" next to Gustav the V's name. I've marked the remainder of the names with check marks, with the exception of one that I've marked with a "?"

It seems that as part of the AAU's presentations, an amateur athlete named Avery Brundage is being called to offer testimony. As a sportswriter, I know the name. Brundage is a star amateur athlete himself and was a teammate of Thorpe's on the 1912 Olympic team. In fact, many in the sporting circles thought he would prevail as the great

American hope in the Games of the V Olympiad in Stockholm, yet he finished only sixth in the pentathlon and fifteenth in the decathlon events. I suppose there was some consolation in the fact that he won the U.S. all-around national title last year, though some sportswriters suggested the victory was a bit hollow since Jim Thorpe, who had been banned from competing, was not among the competitors.

In addition to being a skilled athlete, Brundage is apparently also a very bright and enterprising guy. He graduated magna cum laude with a degree in civil engineering from the University of Illinois several years ago and recently started his own business, aptly titled Avery Brundage Company Builders. The article gives no further information regarding what insight Brundage may bring to this hearing. None of Thorpe's other teammates are on the list, as far as I can see, and I wonder why his testimony might be important. I jot down a few thoughts in my notebook; actually a few scattered words. I make a mental note to observe their interaction during the hearing—whether they make eye contact, exchange a greeting, tense at the sight of one another. I've read a few comments about Brundage's supposed feelings about Thorpe, but I've seen enough at this point to know not to believe everything I read.

Judge Parker, whom I haven't met and doubtfully ever will, enters and calls the court to order. Gus Welch, who has been sitting and conversing with Jim and Iva Thorpe, looks comfortable and at ease when called to take the stand. Knowing what I now do about him, I think I understand why. Having a beef with the Carlisle Indian School administration regarding alleged transgressions made him justifiably ill-at-ease walking through the streets of Carlisle. Today, he appears in this courtroom on behalf of his best friend, and he and the people of Carlisle are on the same side. Attending law school can't hurt his comfort level either.

After being sworn in, Welch sits square-shouldered and straight in his seat, looking directly into the eyes of Parker.

"Mr. Welch, what is your relationship with Mr. Jim Thorpe?" Parker begins.

"Jim Thorpe is my best friend." Welch replies directly to the question, without grandeur or fanfare.

"How did you come to meet Mr. Thorpe?" Parker wants to know. I get that the law is precise and all, but surely there are more relevant questions that the entire court doesn't already know the answers to. Not eating a full breakfast has made me fidgety already and more than a tad cynical.

Gus goes on to explain that he is a full-blooded Chippewa Indian, born in Spooner, Wisconsin. He attended the Carlisle Indian School and, at five-feet, eleven-inches, and 152 pounds, was the school's starting quarterback.

"Jim and I played football together in 1911 and 1912. We played both offense and defense. We also played the entire game. I believe there were only two or three games a season we would have a substitute," Gus informs the court, smiling in Jim's direction as he recalls their glory days.

Thorpe gives a sort of nod, but he's not smiling. The memories, I think, must be bittersweet.

"It seems to me that an athlete of such prominence might be resented by fellow teammates," Parker comments. Welch says nothing. "Was Mr. Thorpe resented by his teammates?" the judge asks.

"I hadn't realized you were looking for a response, Your Honor," Welch quickly says. "No, sir. There wasn't a player on our team that resented Jim. Quite the opposite, as a matter of fact. Everyone respected him and loved playing on the same team with him. We all loved winning," he adds.

"Was Mr. Thorpe a good teammate, Mr. Welch?"

"He was the best teammate I have ever played with, sir."

"How so?"

"Jim had the biggest heart of any man I've ever known. He was always willing to help any of the newcomers and I don't think he could have been any more co-operative," Welch explains.

Parker nods. "Mr. Welch, you will understand if I ask a few more personal questions." It's not exactly a question.

"Of course, Your Honor," Welch replies without hesitation.

"During your football days at the Indian School with Mr. Thorpe, did he ever behave in an unsportsmanlike manner?"

"I am not sure what you mean by 'unsportsmanlike,' sir, but I would have to say 'no.'"

"Did Mr. Thorpe ever conduct himself inappropriately, get into trouble, and try to cover it up? To the best of your knowledge, did he ever cheat in a game, or on a test, for that matter?"

Welch clears his throat a little, a sign to me that he is preparing for a lengthy answer.

"By the time Jim and I began playing together, he had been in and out of the Carlisle Indian School twice. He confided in me that the school was the best thing that could have ever happened to him. Sure, he had a few gripes about some of the regulations. We all did. But Jim Thorpe is a born leader and expressed his concerns, openly and honestly. He didn't ever try to hide anything. He didn't have to. We were always prepared for our football games and we always knew the rules. No one on the football field ever questioned that. Even when we played our weekly scrimmages at Dickinson, where we always slaughtered them, games were fun and we were all still speaking to each other when they were over. People don't do that if they think you're cheating,"

Welch could probably go on, but Parker interjects. "If, as you say, Mr. Thorpe and the football team were always prepared and knew the rules, why would he not know that playing professional baseball during the summer season would change his amateur status?" The question seems to trouble everyone in the courtroom, including me. But not Gus Welch. He looks the judge square in the eye.

"We knew the rules, Your Honor, because they were taught to us. We were accustomed to getting some kind of money when we were playing at the school so that we could live. No one ever told Jim that playing and getting paid whatever it was that they paid him in that Eastern Carolina league made him a professional. How could he break a rule that he was never once taught?" Welch says rhetorically.

Judge Parker stares at Welch for a minute, maybe more, and then asks him what his current status is. "I am studying at Dickinson School of Law, Your Honor. Plan to be a member of the graduating class of 1917."

Parker doesn't even attempt to conceal a smile, wishes him well in his studies and, probably, good riddance from the stand. I think the judge is trying hard to maintain being tough while still being fair. All Welch's testimony has done is muddy the waters a bit more for him. If a man isn't aware that he is cheating, should what he did still be considered as such, and should he still be penalized for it?

This time, when Glen Warner is called, the questions are focused on Thorpe's training for the 1912 Olympic Games.

"Jim had a very relaxed attitude and approach to training," Warner explains. "But that is not to say that he was lazy. He just really was a natural. He really was—is—that good. He didn't have to work as hard, physically, as many of the other athletes. Some of his teammates—on the Olympic team, not my football team—resented him for it. On my squad, teammates support one another. The better your teammate does, the better your team performs. At Carlisle, Jim had nothing but his teammates' respect because he earned it."

As Warner recounts for the judge his rigorous and advanced training table for his football program, Parker again interjects. "This sounds like quite an extensive and, may I add, expensive program, Mr. Warner. How was the school able to afford it?"

Warner reveals many of the details he divulged to me my first night in town, acknowledging that the Indian school's athletic program made sufficient profit to offer high-caliber training to his athletes, as well as to provide them with clothing and other miscellaneous items.

"So, would you say your athletes were monetarily compensated then?" Parker inquires.

"Well, compensated, yes, but not on a significant scale. Just enough to sustain their needs," Warner replies.

In his testimony, Warner reveals that much of Thorpe's training had been part of his track and football practices at the school. Distance running, broad jumping, hurdling, pole vaulting, and discus throwing were all part of the norm.

"He never threw a javelin until two months before the Olympics, though, which is probably why he placed fourth in that event in the Pentathlon." Pop smiles. "He came in first in everything else in that one," he adds. The courtroom bursts into applause, the gavel sounds and the ovation ceases.

The judge asks Warner if there is anything else he would like to add before we recess for lunch. Pop pauses for a moment, glancing at the section where Sullivan and other members of the AAU and IOC are sitting. Then he looks out at the public gathering in the courtroom.

"The Olympic team that Jim Thorpe was part of was not a team in the true sense of the word. These men came together because of their considerable talents and for a common goal, but they had none of the ties that bind a true team. Each man wanted his own talent to be acknowledged, and rightfully so. But, once teammates start to compete amongst themselves, the team falls apart and the competition becomes about the individual. No one in their right mind would want to compete against Jim as an individual. Anyone who wants to win would want him on their side. And anyone who has spent even a day with him knows the man is honest, loyal, and no cheat."

I think Warner has completed another fine précis and I'm about to bolt out of my seat and straight to the Hamilton, vowing never again to skip breakfast before a hearing. But Pop continues on.

"If Jim Thorpe thought that playing baseball during 1909–1910 made him a professional, why didn't he just pursue a professional career at that point? Why did he return to Carlisle and play football, instead? It is obvious to me that he wasn't being paid a significant enough sum to think he was a pro." These are some of the same questions I had asked myself when the story first presented itself. I lean back in my seat and can almost swear Pop looking right at me.

Judge Parker pauses briefly to absorb Warner's take on the story and then recesses the court for lunch. A glance at my watch tells me the timing might be right for the Hamilton. I see the familiar face of yesterday's lunch companion, who seems to be in a hurry, but greets me warmly.

"I was hoping to meet you again, Mr. Murphy," Fredrik says, shaking my hand firmly.

"Want to grab a bite with me?" I inquire, but Fredrik shakes his head.

"I am having lunch sent to King Gustav in a private room at the courthouse. I told him about your American hot dogs and he is eager to taste them."

I laugh out loud at the thought of royalty consuming America's most casual cuisine. Fredrik stops my laughter mid-throat when he tells me that King Gustav requests my presence as his dining companion this evening at the Molly.

"I told him about your kindness to me, your admiration of Mr. Thorpe, and your enjoyment of tennis," Fredrik explains. "I also told him that you appeared to be a man of principle. That is of the utmost importance to the King."

I thank Fredrik for the compliment, graciously accept the dinner invitation and, later, ponder how the heck I'm supposed to act while eating with a King, while I shovel down my lunch.

When I return to the courtroom, I seek out Pop Warner. I want to ask him if he knew Thorpe was playing for the Carolina league at the time, or if he learned it later on, when Thorpe returned to Carlisle. I look around, but to no avail. Maybe I don't need to know the answers to these questions after all. It is not Pop Warner or his judgment on trial. It is the amateur status of Jim Thorpe.

A man in his late twenties, with a solid athletic build, takes the stand. When the judge asks Avery Brundage about his background, he details his accomplishments as an amateur athlete, including his recent All-Around National Title, which is a specialty event somewhat similar to a decathlon.

"Are you still competing in amateur sports, Mr. Brundage?"

"I am proud of my physical attributes and capabilities and will continue to compete as a proud member of the AAU," he replies. I look over at Sullivan and the rest. You can tell that Brundage has just secured his place in their future ranks.

"How do you know Jim Thorpe, Mr. Brundage?" Parker is asking.

"I was a member of the 1912 U.S. Olympic team. Mr. Thorpe was also on that team," Brundage replies. The phrasing surprises me, but after Pop Warner's words of wisdom about what being a team means, it shouldn't have.

"Did you and Mr. Thorpe train for and compete in the same events?" Parker asks.

"We competed in several of the same events. I wouldn't exactly say that we trained together, however."

Parker doesn't even have to ask him to elaborate. "On the boat ride to Sweden, most of us trained and practiced hard every day, but Mr. Thorpe spent a lot of time sleeping or lazing around in a hammock, just staring out at sea," Brundage says.

At Judge Parker's request, he goes on to relate stories about the atmosphere of the Olympic Games and various Olympic events. The games were very successful in the eyes of the U.S. athletes, who won a total of 63 medals: twenty-five gold, nineteen silver, and nineteen bronze.

"I was honored to participate in the Games of the V Olympiad and proud of my accomplishments as an athlete," Brundage concludes.

Judge Parker allows the spectators their moment of personal expression, then leans forward in his chair, intertwining his fingers, before resting them on the desk in front of him.

"Mr. Brundage, one final question. Being an amateur athlete and obviously well-informed individual, you are surely familiar with other athletes who have played ball during the summer seasons, likely under assumed names. I would not ask you to divulge this information publicly. I will ask if you think Mr. Thorpe was aware that he was considered a professional when he played for the Eastern Carolina League and then afterwards participated in the Olympic Games."

"I think that ignorance is no excuse, Your Honor," Brundage replies curtly. Parker dismisses him from the stand amidst a chorus of jeers from the crowd.

The judge bangs his gavel and demands order, but with slightly less vehemence than he has done so previously. Once the spectators have quieted down, the court clerk calls for "His Highness, King Gustav V of Sweden." The crowd can't seem to help itself. From the average townsperson to the most seasoned among the reporters, we all turn reflexively toward the door.

I doubt any of us has ever seen a king. Well, maybe some of the European press, but certainly none of the Americans. I have to admit that it's a bit exciting—I'm close enough to reach out and touch the sleeve of his coat. Gustav is preceded into the room by Fredrik, whose eyes cut briefly in my direction as he maintains his professional demeanor.

"Your Highness," Parker begins, "thank you for taking the time to attend this hearing. I hope that you can shed some light on the 1912 Olympic Games, and specifically on James Thorpe's participation."

"I will try," replies Gustav with a lilting Scandinavian accent. His bearing can only be called regal—he has about the best posture I've ever seen, and even this heat hasn't softened the sharp creases in his uniform. Doesn't royalty sweat?

"We were, of course, quite pleased to host the Olympic games in Stockholm. I had heard of Mr. Thorpe's athletic accomplishments and was rather anxious to witness them in person. I was, naturally, not disappointed.

"As you know, 1912 was the first time the pentathlon was included in the program. It is also the first time any Olympic games employed the use of a public address system and of photographic equipment to record close finishes." He says this last with pride, and who can blame him? Stockholm was also the first host city to use mechanized timing devices to record speed and distance.

"Your Highness, can you tell me something about Mr. Thorpe's participation in the games?"

"Because I knew of his reputation, I was, as I have said, quite anxious to see Mr. Thorpe's performance. I knew that he would compete in the pentathlon and decathlon, the two most demanding events of the games. In the pentathlon, he placed first in the running broad jump, the 200-metre dash, the 1500-metre run, and throwing the discus. In each case, he was far ahead of the competition. The only event he did not win was the javelin, for which he came in fourth, as you heard earlier. However, he won the overall event and, later that day, I presented him with a gold medal."

Through some sort of royal telepathy, Fredrik appears from the witness seats to hand the king a glass of water and a sheet of paper. Gustav takes a tidy sip, returns the glass to Fredrik, looks briefly at the paper, and continues speaking. The crowd seems enchanted by his accent and descriptive language.

"The decathlon began five days later. The first day was very wet, with heavy rains beginning in the morning. On that day, Mr. Thorpe was third in the 100-metre dash and second in the running broad jump. But he was first in throwing the shot put.

"On the next day, in fine weather, he was first in the high jump and the 100-metre hurdle. In that race, his time was just more than fifteen seconds, a feat which I would never have believed a human capable of accomplishing. He also scored fourth in the 400-metre run.

"By the third day, we were all anxious to see whether he could keep up this astonishing performance. He placed second in the discus event and third in the pole vault. But when it came to the 1,500-metre run, he beat even his own performance of just days earlier. His overall score was far ahead of the second place winner, and I presented his second gold medal."

"Were other prizes awarded, in addition to the medals?" asks the judge.

"Yes, there were also two trophies. For the pentathlon, I presented Mr. Thorpe with a bronze bust of my likeness," Gustav replies, with no apparent trace of humility. "The trophy for the decathlon was a chalice in the form of a Viking ship, presented by Czar Nicholas of Russia."

"Thank you, Your Highness," Judge Parker says. "Again, I appreciate your willingness to offer testimony today. You may step down."

As expected, Fredrik seemingly flies across the room to escort the king up the aisle.

The clerk calls Moses Friedman. Acknowledging that he is still under oath, Friedman takes the stand. Judge Parker asks him to describe the events that welcomed the athletes upon their return from Stockholm.

"Your Honor, you may recall that the entire country was quite proud of our boys," Friedman begins. "And especially in Carlisle, we felt that they deserved a real heroes' welcome. The town held a parade on August 16 to honor Jim Thorpe, Glenn Warner, and Lewis Tewanima, another Indian student who won a silver medal at the games."

"So the athletes were well received by the town?"

"Yes, sir, absolutely. The crowds must have been ten deep along High Street. I think the entire town came out for the parade. People were cheering and waving, the band played—it was quite an event. The parade ended at the Indian School, where I greeted Warner, Thorpe, and Tewanima, and officially thanked them on behalf of the school and the town for their outstanding performances at the Olympic Games."

"Thank you, Mr. Friedman," Parker says. "I think we have a clear understanding of the town's appreciation for its athletes. You may step down."

Banging the gavel once, the judge says, "This hearing is adjourned for today, and will resume tomorrow at 9:00."

"All rise," states the clerk, and we all stand as the judge leaves the bench.

It's 4:30, so I've got plenty of time to get ready for my dinner with King Gustav. When I get back to the hotel, I go directly to the front desk and ask Jimmy to send someone to my room to pick up my suit for pressing.

"Certainly, Mr. Murphy. When do you need it returned?"

"By seven, Jimmy. I have to wear it to dinner tonight at eight. I hope that's not too much of an inconvenience."

"Absolutely not," he replies cheerfully. "I'll instruct the laundry to take care of it right away."

I'll tell Jimmy about the dinner tomorrow. Right now I want to take a nap, but my head is filled with thoughts of the day's hearing and what it will be like to dine with the king. At six I give up and take a shower—I still can't get over what a pleasant experience it is—and wait for my suit to be returned.

At 6:30 there's a knock at the door, and I figure Jimmy pushed the laundry into even faster service. Opening the door, I'm surprised to see Fredrik.

"May I speak with you for a few moments?" he asks.

"Of course, please come in."

"There are a few items of protocol that we must review before you meet His Highness," Fredrik says.

I'm actually glad he's here, because wondering how to behave in the presence of royalty had been part of what kept me from napping. He explains that dinner will be served in the King's suite. Fredrik will make the introduction, effectively presenting me, and I will bow from the waist. He demonstrates a bow, in case I'm uncertain. I will not sit until the King asks me to. Basically, I won't do much of anything until the King asks (or tells?) me to, or does it first himself. I'm not to eat or drink until Gustav has begun (I'm starting to wonder if Fredrik has to taste his food). And I will, of course, address him as "your Highness." The meal is being prepared according to the King's wishes and I can only hope that we won't be dining on some obscure Swedish delicacy that I don't recognize.

I thank Fredrik for the lesson and immediately start to worry about spilling my soup or committing some other faux pas. Well, there's no point in thinking about it, I suppose. When my suit arrives, I dress carefully, and kill some time by practicing facial expressions in the mirror. I try variations of humility, deference, polite smiles, genteel laughter—and yes, I even practice bowing. Oh brother, this is going to be quite an evening.

I reach the royal suite at precisely eight o'clock. I barely knock when Fredrik opens the door and welcomes me. King Gustav is standing at the desk, looking at a sheaf of papers.

"Your Highness," says Fredrik, "may I present Mr. Bud Murphy, reporter for the *Evening News*."

I bow, and Gustav inclines his head almost imperceptibly. "Your Highness, it is indeed an honor to meet you."

The king is an impressive man. His height is accentuated by his excellent posture and his Nordic coloring, with blond hair and pale blue eyes, adds to his distinctive look. He is in his early fifties and is remarkably fit. In fact, he looks like a tennis player—tall and lean, and probably quite agile. And the uniform doesn't hurt the image, either. Trying not to stare, I count at least fifteen medals across his left breast. The jacket is richly adorned with gold leaf on the epaulets, high collar, and stiff cuffs, and a satin sash crosses it from the right shoulder. Gee, what does he wear when he's relaxing at home? Do kings relax at home?

"Mr. Murphy, Fredrik has told me of your most amiable conversation yesterday. He was pleased to meet a reporter who is a true fan of sports and who seems to agree with our opinion of Mr. Thorpe. Please, let us sit."

Gustav moves to a lavishly set table in an alcove, and Fredrik holds out a chair for the king. Once he is seated, Fredrik does the same for me. A waiter appears from another room to pour wine for the king, who tastes it and nods. The waiter pours glasses for both of us, and I wait for Gustav to take his first real sip before raising my glass. The wine is excellent, white and crisp, a far cry from what I am accustomed to drinking.

The king speaks. "I imagine that you were in the courtroom today, Mr. Murphy."

"Yes, I was, Your Highness. It was very interesting to hear your personal account of Jim Thorpe's performance at the Olympics."

"Ah, it was fascinating to have been witness to such accomplishments. As a sports enthusiast, you can appreciate the magnitude of Thorpe's achievements. I certainly never expected that one man could consistently excel at so many different sports."

Gustav smiles, and his entire countenance changes. The posture is still perfect, the uniform is still impeccable, but he becomes much more human and even seems to relax a bit.

"Do you like the wine?" he asks, "or would you prefer something else, perhaps beer?"

To be honest, I'd love a beer, but there's no way in hell I'm going to ask for one. The king could drink poison and I'd raise a glass of the same. "Thank you; the wine is perfect," I reply.

"So, I understand from Fredrik that you enjoy playing tennis," says Gustav.

"Yes, Your Highness, I do. Although I don't get to play as often as I'd like to, I find the game exhilarating."

"As do I. In fact, I'm quite passionate about it." He chuckles. "I think many of my countrymen would be surprised. But I agree with your assessment of the game as exhilarating. It gets the blood pumping through one's veins. I saw the Renshaw brothers play at Wimbledon and was amazed by their skill. Whether playing separately or as doubles partners, they were masters on the court."

Fortunately I've heard of Ernest and William Renshaw, British twins who won thirteen titles between 1881 and '89. We chat pleasantly for a few minutes about the brothers' careers and about May Sutton, an American who was the first overseas winner at Wimbledon, claiming the Ladies' Singles title in 1905.

The king smiles and says, "In fact, from Pennsylvania I will travel to Rhode Island, to see the famous Newport Casino. I have heard that it is an excellent court."

Thanking my lucky stars to be a New Englander, I tell Gustav everything I know about Newport tennis, which is a considerable amount. In fact, the conversation is going so well that I barely register the fact that I'm eating snails. Why can't rich people eat normal food?

While I'm busily practicing my table manners, the king returns to the subject of Jim Thorpe. "I truly hope that this hearing brings the desired outcome," he says with feeling. "I do not hesitate to say that I was appalled when I read of Thorpe's treatment. For the Amateur Athletic Association to so quickly judge him was reprehensible. This man, Sullivan, seems to take too personal an interest. A man should not be treated as a hero and then be vilified for an innocent act. If I could rule, his medals would be returned and he would receive formal apologies from all involved."

Our main course consists of perfectly cooked lamb chops, accompanied by buttery potatoes and tender asparagus. For this dish, the waiter pours a red wine that feels like velvet on my palate. This more than makes up for the escargot.

By this time I'm feeling much more comfortable in the royal presence, and am not afraid to speak. "Your Highness, I can say honestly that when I came to Carlisle, I was fairly neutral in this matter. Of course, I had the utmost respect and admiration for Thorpe's talent, but as a reporter, I was skeptical about his innocence. But the people who support him have been very forthcoming, and I've had the opportunity to talk with Mr. Warner as well as Thorpe's wife and best friend. After that, and seeing Thorpe himself in court, I have to admit that I've moved fully into his corner. I also hope the judge rules in his favor."

Our meal concludes with a dessert of angel food cake topped with fresh berries and cream and coffee. When I comment on the wonderful meal, the king says, "The staff here has done a fine job of preparing an excellent meal." He smiles, almost boyishly, before continuing. "But I will admit that I am indebted to you for introducing Fredrik to the hot dog. What a splendid lunch it made today." He laughs heartily. "Most unroyal, I am sure, but sometimes even a king must do something solely for the pleasure it brings. I think we will have another tomorrow!"

Thinking we've reached the end of the evening, I'm surprised when Gustav suggests that we move to the comfortable armchairs near the window. He calls for Fredrik, who brings two snifters of brandy and hands the king several photographs.

The king shows me pictures of the Olympic trophies. The bust of Gustav looks to weigh a ton, being solid bronze and quite large. And the decathlon trophy from Russia, studded with all types of jewels, must be worth a small fortune. I comment that Thorpe must have been fairly overwhelmed to receive these, in addition to his gold medals.

"I believe he was," says the king. "But I also believe that he deserves them. As I told him when I presented the trophy for the pentathlon, he is the greatest athlete in the world."

We discuss sports in general as we finish our brandy. At 10:30, I take my leave of the royal suite, thanking King Gustav for his hospitality. He extends his hand and thanks me for an evening of pleasant conversation. Shaking his hand, I am again amazed at the turns this trip has taken. I bow one last time and return to my room.

CHAPTER 8

When I awaken on Wednesday, I take a few minutes to revel in the memory of the previous evening's events. I had dinner with a king! A private audience, to be exact—a command performance. I mentally review the entire experience to see whether I committed any social errors, and blessedly can't think of a single mistake. I think the night went beautifully and can't wait to get home to share this story with my father.

But for today, it's back to the business of Jim Thorpe. I tell myself not to gloat over last night's good fortune, but I feel particularly energized after my royal encounter and dress quickly to head for the dining room. After yesterday, there's no way I'm skipping breakfast this morning.

Jimmy looks up from his post as I descend the stairs to the lobby.

"Good morning, Mr. Murphy. I hope you had a pleasant dinner. Was the suit pressed to your satisfaction?"

I take a moment to realize how good Jimmy is at his job. Nothing gets past him.

"The suit was perfect, Jimmy. Thanks for taking care of that for me." Remembering my personal admonition not to make too much of the dinner, I hesitate briefly before continuing. But I like Jimmy, and know he'll genuinely appreciate the story.

"Dinner was more than pleasant, in fact. I was lucky enough to be the guest of King Gustav."

As professional as Jimmy is, even he can't hide his surprise. For a second I think the poor kid's swallowed his tongue.

"You had dinner with the king?" he nearly whispers. "No one mentioned seeing him in the dining room, where did you eat?"

"In his suite," I reply. "It was just the two of us. I'd struck up a conversation with his assistant the day before yesterday and he told the king about it. Turns out we actually have a couple of things in common, and he wanted to discuss Jim Thorpe."

"Holy mackerel," Jimmy says quietly. "Were you nervous?"

"I was at first, but King Gustav is very nice, and really put me at ease. He's easy to talk to, once you get over the fact that he's royalty."

"Gee, Mr. Murphy," Jimmy says almost reverently. "You sure are a lucky man. I thought it was neat when you had dinner with Pop Warner, but now a king too. Bet you can't wait to see who you meet next!"

As I grab a newspaper and head to the dining room, I find myself wondering the same thing.

Waiting for my pancakes, I open the paper to the line-up for today's hearing. And read the names of two men I sure would like to meet, but for all the wrong reasons. Leading off the hearing will be testimony by Charles Clancy and Roy Johnson, the pair who effectively stole my thunder by breaking the Thorpe story.

Something makes me pull my notebook and pencil from my pocket and begin writing. Not a story, or even notes for one. Just some thoughts about my experiences since I arrived in Carlisle nearly a week ago. I jot down my actual assignment: cover Thorpe hearing. Period. An assignment that I know, for plenty of the other reporters in town, means nothing more than sitting in the courtroom every day taking notes and writing a standard piece about the testimony. Whatever they do when court isn't in session is their business.

But for me, this has turned into much more than a run-of-the-mill assignment. Continuing to make notes as I eat my breakfast, I wonder if any other reporters have had the privilege of the company I've been keeping. And I'm pretty sure no one else has dined with the king.

Pondering this, I realize that Clancy and Johnson aren't that important any longer. Yes, their actions had an impact on my life and

I was upset about it for a long time. But that's over now. I've gotten to meet some fascinating people, and I've learned an awful lot, about more than just what happened to Jim Thorpe.

And to be perfectly honest, Roy Johnson can have his breaking story. I intend to make the current Thorpe story the best I've ever written. I've been lucky enough to have gotten some exclusive interviews, and my mind is already abuzz with the series of articles I can spin from what's become a fascinating assignment.

And I'm pretty sure I'd hate to be either Clancy or Johnson on that witness stand today, testifying in front of a pro-Thorpe crowd.

As I walk to the courthouse, it strikes me that I barely even notice the heat any longer. Guess I'm getting pretty comfortable here in Carlisle. I take my seat and notice that the usual crowd is assembled in the courtroom and overflowing into the corridor as the clerk calls the room to order.

Judge Parker takes the bench and the clerk immediately calls Charles Clancy to the stand. Once Clancy is sworn in, the judge begins his questioning.

"Mr. Clancy, how do you know Jim Thorpe?"

"He played baseball on two of my teams in the Carolina League, Your Honor."

"And when was this?"

"In both 1909 and 1910," Clancy replies without hesitation.

"Were you aware of Mr. Thorpe's participation in the Olympic Games of 1912?" asks the judge.

"I was."

"And why did you not come forward with this information at that time?"

"Well, sir, I didn't recognize the name. Of course I knew about Thorpe's Olympic wins, and saw a couple of pictures of him in the paper, but I didn't realize he was the same man who'd played in my league."

"When did you realize who he is?" Parker prompts.

I reflexively tense up, waiting for Clancy to describe the game where we first met.

"I attended a football game between Notre Dame and the Carlisle Indians, and I recognized Thorpe then. That was in the fall of 1912, after the Olympics."

Parker seems to consider this for a moment, then asks, "And what did you do with this information, Mr. Clancy?"

"Actually, Your Honor, I didn't think all that much of it at first," Clancy replies. "I mean, I was more surprised than anything, to realize that I'd had this world-famous athlete on my team, but I didn't initially even think about the implications of his having played professional ball."

"So how did this become an issue?" asks the judge.

I feel as though I've stopped breathing. I realize that this is what I've been waiting for. More than anything, I want Clancy's answer to this one question, but I'm afraid to think about why.

"The man I went to the game with was a retired sports reporter," he continues. "And when I told him that I recognized Thorpe from my team, he got very excited, and started talking about how the Olympics are only for amateur athletes, and that this could turn out to be a huge scandal."

The spectators seem to lean forward as one, waiting for Clancy to go on. I look over at the witness section and see that Thorpe is sitting as rigidly as a statue, and his wife is gripping his arm. Both are staring straight at Clancy.

"That got me thinking," he continues. "And by halftime I was pretty much convinced that he was right, that Thorpe definitely should not have competed in the Olympics after playing professional ball. And then my friend met another reporter he used to work with and told him about our conversation. He even encouraged this other fellow to pursue the story and the reporter and I agreed that he'd call me to talk more about it."

And right now, "this other fellow" couldn't be more relieved that he'd missed that big break. Yes, I'd wanted that story badly, but today I wouldn't trade places with Roy Johnson for any amount of fame.

"And what happened next?" asks the judge.

"Well, I talked with the reporter a couple of times. He was very interested in the story, but wanted all sorts of documentation of the facts—my team roster, any photos of the players, payment receipts, and he asked me so many questions. I knew the story was important and agreed that the public should know about it, but I was spending a couple of months with family in Massachusetts, and all that paperwork was back in my office in Eastern Carolina. I suppose I could have asked my assistant to send it up to me, but was busy with other things and just didn't get around to it.

"In the end, though, I met another reporter at a local football game. We got to talking about different players, and Thorpe's name came up. I told him about Thorpe playing ball for me, and the guy nearly went nuts. He kept saying it would be the story of the century, and he really pursued me. And the next thing I knew, the story was on the front page."

The judge dismisses Clancy, and the clerk summons Roy R. Johnson to the stand.

"Mr. Johnson," Parker begins, "what did you do after Mr. Clancy told you that Jim Thorpe played professional ball for him?"

"I contacted Mr. Clancy the next day to interview him further. He told me several stories about Thorpe's antics in Eastern Carolina and confirmed that Thorpe did indeed get paid to play."

Judge Parker asks, "Did you request any documentation from Mr. Clancy?"

"No sir," says Johnson. "I was comfortable with his statements and, since I knew how important the story could be, I felt that I had enough information to print it. I didn't want to waste time."

Waste time. What a joke. I'm more convinced than ever that Johnson wasn't the most scrupulous reporter, and he's probably no better as an editor. Anyone worth his paycheck wouldn't consider it a waste of time to research a story that could ruin a man's life.

"I was pretty persistent," Johnson says. "I knew that this story would be huge, and I wanted it for the *Worcester Telegram*. So I kept after Clancy until he agreed to let me run it. That took about two weeks, and we went to print on January 22. There were five follow-up articles after that."

As the judge dismisses the witness, I find that my emotions are roiling. Although I think Johnson is a louse, I'm no longer sorry about being scooped. Instead, I'm outraged by what appears to be his total lack of concern for anything but his damned story. He couldn't be bothered to verify the facts and obviously couldn't care less about the repercussions. Yeah, he knew the story could be important—for his own self-serving purposes.

Next on the stand is James Sullivan of the AAU.

"Mr. Sullivan, tell me how you became aware of the charges that Jim Thorpe played baseball as a professional," the judge demands.

"As Secretary of the Amateur Athletic Union, I was made aware of the story that ran in the *Worcester Telegram*. A member of our board who'd seen the article brought it to my attention."

I still can't figure out how Sullivan could have been completely unaware of Thorpe's playing history. For crying out loud, Thorpe applied to the AAU *after* he left Carolina. Since he was already a rising star in amateur football with an eye on the Olympics, it's hard to believe that no one in the AAU paid closer attention.

"And what action did you take after reading the article?" Parker asks.

"I immediately wrote a letter to Mr. Friedman, the superintendent of the Carlisle Indian School, asking him to question Mr. Thorpe about the allegations."

"What was the response to your letter?"

"Mr. Friedman wrote back at once," Sullivan says. "He informed me that the school authorities conducted a thorough investigation, and that Thorpe admitted having played for two professional baseball teams in the Carolina League. I also received a letter from Thorpe acknowledging the facts, which he read to the court several days ago."

The judge asks, "And based on these letters, what action did you take?"

"It was decided that the AAU would retroactively withdraw Jim Thorpe's status as an amateur athlete. I also contacted the International Olympic Committee to recommend that they do the same. After conducting their own investigation, the IOC also declared Thorpe a professional and stripped him of his titles, medals, and awards. He was required to return the medals and awards to the Olympic Committee in Switzerland."

"Thank you, Mr. Sullivan; you may be seated," the judge says. Addressing the spectators, he continues, "I have now heard all the testimony in this case, and will render my decision tomorrow. This hearing is adjourned."

The room immediately erupts with noise. Reporters rush toward the witness box, jostling spectators out of the way as they fire questions at Thorpe. But I can't bring myself to join the throng. What can he possibly say, except that he hopes the judge rules in his favor? Leave the poor man alone—he's got to be nervous enough knowing that tomorrow he'll finally learn whether this nightmare is over.

While my colleagues press on, I head the other way, out of the courtroom. I think briefly about trying to get a quote from Sullivan, but honestly, I want out of this room, away from the noise. There's still tomorrow for that.

Right now, I'm thirsty, and I find myself turning into Wilkins Tavern, just a few doors from the hotel. The Molly is grand, but today I don't feel grand at all. I want to be in my own element, where I can have a beer and talk with the locals, and we can all try to convince ourselves that the judge will rule our way. Our way...I think I've got Carlisle, and Thorpe, in my blood.

CHAPTER 9

During yesterday's hearing, Judge Parker announced that he would make his decision today. I've been lying awake for almost an hour already this morning, part of me eager to have the hearing come to a close, though only just to know the outcome of the reinstatement of Jim Thorpe's medals. A much bigger part of me is reluctant for all of this to end. The story has become much more than a sports item, and I will be hard-pressed to find another that will match its worth.

I look around my room, articles of clothing strewn in various places though housekeeping has done a good job of keeping me in order. A guy could get used to this. A guy *did* get used to this. And, in less than twenty-four hours, this guy will be leaving it all behind and returning to the quiet reality of his real life. And, if justice prevails, Jim Thorpe will be able to do the same, though his real life will undoubtedly continue to be far from quiet and far more eventful than mine.

I envision the gleam in Thorpe's eyes should Judge Parker rule in his favor, vindicating him from these trumped up charges, the applause in the courtroom, the embraces he will exchange with Iva, Pop Warner, and Gus Welch, and the pride he will feel all over again when those Olympic medals are once more draped around his neck. I know, from yesterday's presentations, that, of course, the medals and awards are not here in Carlisle, though what a magnificent sight that would be. And I know too that I am getting way ahead of myself. There is just as good a chance that Parker's decision will leave everything exactly the way it is.

Lying here will not postpone the day. It will just make me late, so I put aside my well-used notebook in which I've unconsciously been writing story leads. I can't think of a worse way to jinx the outcome of this hearing, so I rip out the pages, crumple and shred them into indecipherable pieces and tell myself I'm not the least bit superstitious as I head for my lucky shower, as I now call this new-age contraption that has been the start of many a fortuitous day since I arrived here in Carlisle.

The shower was invigorating, but did nothing to wash away the anxiety that accompanies this day, so I seek the company of someone else likely feeling the same as I do. One look at Jimmy behind the front desk and I know that I've found my man. He seems happy to see me, but not quite his good-natured self. Pensive, I think, is the mood and word of the day.

"Morning, Mr. Murphy," is the best Jimmy can do this morning. Talking to this young man, I realize, was the true beginning of my lucky streak in Carlisle.

"How you holding up today, Jimmy?" I ask, knowing that his perspective about this case is based partially on his dedication to his local hero. His local hero did nothing to warrant anything less than his admiration, at least from what I've seen and heard.

"Heck, I'm okay. I'm not the one I'm worried about, though. Can't imagine how Jim Thorpe must be feeling this morning," Jimmy replies. "What's he gonna do if the judge doesn't give him back those medals?" he asks.

And, though I know it's a rhetorical question, I find myself wanting to allay Jimmy's fears without giving him false hope. "He'll do the same thing he's been doing all this time, buddy. He'll play ball and be the best player in the world." I smile, not very convincingly.

"Yeah, but if he loses at this hearing, that's it, Mr. Murphy. At least before, he had hope that things would change and people would know he didn't cheat," Jimmy says solemnly.

I put my hand on the kid's shoulder and muster every bit of conviction inside me when I say, "People already know Jim Thorpe is no cheat. They don't need a judge or medals to tell them that. And there is always hope, Jimmy." He seems more relaxed with that, and with my work at the front desk done, I am off to the dining room for coffee, though part of me could use a stiff drink.

I didn't even bother to grab a paper. The courtroom lineup is a one-man show today, and I'm not at all interested in any other news of the day. Breakfast is uneventful, and I decide to try to enjoy a cigar on my short jaunt to the courthouse. Stepping out into the bright, hot day, wishing it weren't my last one here, I take in the town of Carlisle. You can feel the tension hanging thick in the air, or is that just the oppressive heat of July bearing down?

I stuff a hand in my pocket to grab a cigar and find the page from the local newspaper that listed the hearing participants. I chuckle at the checks and x's I had marked next to each name. Leaning against the wall of the courthouse, I grab a pencil instead of a cigar and circle the one name on the list that I haven't secured some type of comment from. I was among the throng of reporters who hurled question after question at Pratt, Sullivan, Brundage, and even Roy Johnson. I had already had my own one-on-one interviews with Clancy, though they were a couple of years ago, when things were very different. I have had dinner and enlightening conversations with Warner, Friedman, and the King, and lemonade with Iva Thorpe, who isn't even on this list. So, big hotshot reporter that I am, who did I not get a single, direct comment from?

It isn't that there wasn't opportunity. Most days in the courtroom, Thorpe fielded questions and comments from mobs of reporters who printed his responses as quotes in their stories. My editor had made it a point to bring this up with me. And yes, I could have been among those reporters and done the same. The words were coming from Thorpe's own mouth. But I just couldn't bring myself to be one of the nameless faces he would address. In some odd way, I hoped my lack of presence in the media frenzy would make a difference. Besides, I've been very spoiled by all of the personal contact. A general remark directed at no one in particular wasn't good enough for me. So, unless I get very lucky today, Jim Thorpe will remain unquoted in any of my stories. But I did shower and talk to Jimmy this morning, so who knows?

Then again, Thorpe is the one who could use the luck today, though the outcome of this hearing has nothing to do with luck at all. Reading through the notes I've taken since the hearing began, I am hoping for some of it to come into play. The crowd outside is disappearing into the building, telling me it's almost time to go inside. I decide there's still time for a cigar while the spectators settle in. Those of us in the press have pretty much self-assigned seats by now. Halfway through my smoke, the lobby is almost empty, and I think I had better head upstairs when in walk Pop Warner, Gus Welch, Iva, and Jim Thorpe.

Though I feel like a nervous schoolboy on the inside, I maintain my reporter cool. Pop and Gus reach out to shake my hand while Iva is saying something to Thorpe.

"Nice to see you again, Bud," Pop says. "Today's the big day."

"It sure is," I manage to muster and find myself turning towards Iva and Jim.

"Good luck, Mr. Thorpe," are the only words I have. They are enough. He smiles, shakes my hand, and says, "Thank you, Mr. Murphy." He knows my name. Iva smiles and tells me she hopes my stay in Carlisle was pleasant. I tell her it was and wish I could say more, wish I could have done more, but this brief chance meeting is over as Thorpe is ushered into the courtroom.

I draw a deep breath, collecting myself as I make my way to my seat. I may not have a quote to use in my article, but Jim Thorpe shook my hand and spoke directly to me. Now I can only hope that some of my luck rubs off on him.

Judge Parker enters the courtroom, takes his seat, and announces that he has indeed come to a decision. A hush falls over the crowd.

"On Friday, July 16, this hearing convened to rule as to the status of Jim Thorpe during the 1912 Olympic Games and to the placement of the awards won by Mr. Thorpe at those same games. During the course of this hearing, presentations have been made by all persons and organizations relevant to this matter," Judge Parker begins, and pauses to pick up some papers on his desk.

"Mr. Thorpe was a student at the Carlisle Indian School before participating in the 1912 Olympics. By all accounts, he was s good student, had a respectable record, and was a talented athlete for the school's track and football teams. During the summers of 1909–1910, Mr. Thorpe played baseball for two professional teams in Fayetteville and Rocky Mount, Eastern Carolina. He returned to the Carlisle Indian School in 1911 to continue his studies. While at the school, he registered as a member of the Amateur Athletic Association and began training for the 1912 Olympic Games, which were to be held in Stockholm, Sweden, beginning with opening ceremonies on May 5, 1912 and concluding on July 27, 1912."

Parker continues to read from the outline he has obviously made from the mounds of material on his desk.

"During the 1912 Olympic Games, Jim Thorpe participated in two relatively new multi-event competitions, the pentathlon and decathlon. He won gold medals for the United States of America in both of those events." The judge pauses here, as though he is expecting an interruption, but the audience in this courtroom is frozen in anticipation, not wanting to delay his verdict, even for a moment of recognition of Thorpe's performance.

"In addition to those medals, Mr. Thorpe received two trophies for his accomplishments. In January of 1913, the *Worcester Telegram* published information that Jim Thorpe had played ball for a Eastern Carolina professional baseball team. In a letter dated January 26, 1913, Mr. Thorpe admitted to Mr. Sullivan and the AAU that he had indeed played for the Rocky Mount and Fayetteville baseball teams. Upon receipt of this letter, Mr. Sullivan and the Amateur Athletic Association made the decision to withdraw Mr. Thorpe's status as an amateur at the time of his participation in the 1912 Olympic Games. The International Olympic Committee followed suit and, as a result, Mr. Thorpe was stripped of his awards and medals."

Judge Parker pauses again, looks at the gathering of hopeful supporters in his courtroom, and then at Jim Thorpe.

"Throughout the past five days, I have heard presentations from both sides of this case. I have reviewed letters, documents, and rules and regulations amounting to hundreds of pages, and as ordered by this hearing, I have come to a decision in this matter."

The courtroom is so quiet you can hear a pin drop. I'm not sure anyone would dare to even inhale or exhale a breath. All eyes are focused on Judge Parker, awaiting the decision that could forever alter a man's future and destiny. All eyes, except mine, which are fixed intently on Thorpe as the judge's words fill my ears.

Judge Parker looks in the direction of Jim Thorpe and announces that his decision is the same as that made by the Amateur Athletic Union and the International Olympic Committee. The courtroom still remains quiet, with all eyes looking at Jim as Judge Parker finishes summing up his decision. Jim's head drops and Pop Warner reaches out to comfort him.

The next thing I remember is seeing the locals filing out of the courtroom without saying a word. No one is saying a word. Most of them are looking down at their feet or straight ahead; no expressions are on their faces. They seem stunned by the judge's decision.

CHAPTER 10

I was also stunned by Judge Parker's decision not to restore Jim Thorpe's Olympic medals and records. Even though I knew that this verdict was a possibility, I didn't really believe it would happen. I also felt sad that this was over and I'd soon be leaving the town of Carlisle, where I felt a connection to both the people and the history of Carlisle that I never anticipated. For the moment, I felt the need for some kind of solace that can only be found in the form of multiple shots of whiskey complemented by an occasional ice cold beer. I found that solace at the Wilkins Tavern, where the atmosphere was as glum as I was.

Apparently, the news of the outcome of Thorpe's hearing spread rapidly throughout town. Wilkins Tavern was packed and the people from Carlisle were being very outspoken in their disbelief and disappointment in Judge Parker's decision, while the other reporters were milling about, writing down the locals' comments and adding the finishing touches to the conclusions of their stories. After today, the Thorpe case officially over, like myself, most of the reporters will be boarding the first train out of Carlisle in the morning, heading home or to wherever the next big story takes them. Their collective reason for being here has come to an end. So has mine.

Downing a stiff shot while mentally rehashing the testimony of the ten witnesses called and the hundreds of pages of documents on Judge Parker's desk, I am less than enthused at the prospect of retiring to my room at the Molly to finish and file my story. Though I am hardly ever at a loss for words, I now find myself unable to evoke the choice phrasing and tone I'm usually able to capture. Having a second shot will not help, I know, but I order one anyway.

It's not that I don't understand Parker's decision. Part of my problem is that I actually do understand his reasoning. His job was to decide whether Thorpe should receive his medals back based on his status as either an amateur or professional athlete. He explained that, although he did not feel Mr. Thorpe intentionally participated in the Olympics knowing he was a professional, the order of the court was to rule on Thorpe's actions, not intentions. He had little choice, but to determine that since Thorpe was paid for playing with NC, his athletic status must be considered professional.

Judge Parker said that, once he had reached this conclusion, the next order of business was clear. "Since the rules of the International Olympic Committee explicitly state that the games are for amateurs only, Mr. Thorpe's status as a professional disqualifies him as a participant," Parker said in his ruling. He held up the documents from the IOC, a huge stack of papers with rules and bylaws likely written in a language that people of normal intelligence can't even comprehend.

"It's all right here in black and white," Parker continued in his explanation, adding, "there is no ambiguity on this particular point. I am sure that the IOC will accommodate any request to read their very detailed rules and regulations, though I admit to skimming through inapplicable sections and don't recommend it as leisure reading," he had attempted as a joke.

I recall that none of the courtroom spectators laughed, but I'd noticed something on the faces of a few IOC and AAU committee members after the judge's remark. I couldn't quite put a name to the expression, but it wasn't the smugness I would have expected. It's still bugging me as I contemplate the second shot on the bar in front of me.

I raise my shot glass high and pronounce to no one in particular, "to hell with them all," referring to the members of the AAU and the IOC. The bartender, a guy around my father's age, pours himself a shot from what I'm eyeing as my very own bottle, and asks me to whom we are bidding this undesirable fate. When I tell him, he downs his shot together with me, rests his glass on the bar and begins speaking in a much calmer voice than the rest of the angry and upset local patrons.

"What did anyone really expect, son?" he asks, sounding a lot like my father.

"What? Do you think Jim Thorpe deserved to have those medals taken back?" I ask incredulously.

He pours me another—on the house—and continues. "No, I do not think Jim deserved this. I am not, however, at all surprised that more educated, knowledgeable, and powerful people ultimately got their way. Are you?" he asks.

Now I think he must be related to my father. "Well, no, I guess I'm not surprised at that. But with a judge sorting through the facts, I thought Thorpe might stand a chance," I explain.

He nods. "We all hoped that. Here was a young Indian man looking to better himself, going back to school, competing for his country, and trusting the more informed people around him to help him make decisions. The sad truth is that Jim's ability just didn't sit right with those stiffs, and they found a way to take it all away from him. Not Ed Parker. He did the best he could with what he had to work with. He was just doing his job. It's just too bad he couldn't find a way to undo what those organizations had done."

I sigh, recalling the hefty stack of documents the judge had on his desk throughout the hearing. "Yeah, but I think he tried, though," I say, explaining to the barkeep that I've been covering the hearing and saw the mounds of paperwork Judge Parker had for reference. "He said the rules about being an amateur were clear cut, even tried to joke about how long and boring they were," I continue, and then my voice trails off as I remember something else the judge had said, while simultaneously realizing the bartender just referred to him by first name. "Excuse me, you just said "Ed Parker." You happen to know the judge personally?" I ask casually. I may be leaving town tomorrow, but that's no reason to stop making new friends in Carlisle.

"Ed Parker and I go way back. The name's Pete, pal," the barkeep smiles and extends his hand. I guzzle the third shot that I've been toying with during our conversation, place the empty glass on the bar and shake his hand firmly. "Nice to meet you, Pete," I say, and boy do I mean it.

"If you've got a beef with Ed, you're gonna have to stand in line," he says, half-jokingly.

"To tell you the truth, I feel sort of bad for the judge," I reply carefully. "It couldn't have been easy to make the decision he did."

Pete nods knowingly. "Yeah, that's what he said last night when I spoke with him. The wife invited him for a nice home-cooked meal tonight because he's had such a tough week."

"I'm sure he'll be grateful for that, what with spending all day in court, and going over all those documents must have taken most of his nights," I say with some empathy. "I know this case has taken up most of my time and I'm only a reporter, not the guy who had to make the decision." I am on a mission here, trying hard to get into Pete's good graces, and trying just as hard not to be obvious about it.

Pete studies me carefully. "Mind if I have a look, young fellow?" he gestures at my notebook, lying next to me on the bar.

Now, my notebook is not a thing I generally share with anyone, but something tells me to let Pete have a look. He reads and flips pages, taking his time and not saying a word, except "Hold your horses," to a patron asking for a refill.

When he's through skimming, he pushes the notebook back to me. "Sounds to me like you've made a few friends here in Carlisle, Bud. And sounds to me like the people of Carlisle have found a good friend in you. I don't see any notes in here, though, about Ed's decision or the town's reaction—or your own, for that matter."

"To tell you the truth, I'm having a hard time with that," I reply. "I came right here after the judge's verdict. I have to get back to the hotel pretty soon, file my story, and pack. My train leaves at ten tomorrow morning." While I'm talking, I'm wondering if it's wise to have one last drink.

"Tell you what, Bud," Pete says. "Why don't you blow outta here, go file your story or whatever it is that you do, pack your things, and meet me back here at six p.m. for dinner?"

I look at Pete, a bit confused. "I thought you said you were having dinner at home with Judge Parker?"

Pete grins. "I am. And so are you," he says, and taps gently on the cover of my notebook. "I can see this is more than a job for you.

It's eating at you, and you've still got some questions. I know Ed well enough to know the hearing will be on his mind all night. I think he'll enjoy talking to you. And maybe it'll help settle things for you if you get a chance to meet the key player."

I thank Pete for the invitation and tell him that I would, of course, love to have dinner with him tonight, making a mental note to look for a bakery shop on my way back to the hotel. I don't want to be the unexpected guest who shows up empty-handed.

As I step outside the Wilkins, the air is still hot, but the sunless sky matches the mood of this town. I, however, am thinking that every cloud still has its silver lining. I've already met a King, so why wouldn't I have thought I'd meet the judge?

Looking back, I'm still amazed at just how bright that silver lining turned out to be. Dinner with Pete's family and Judge Parker was even better than I'd hoped. Pete's wife, Mary, was very gracious, showing no surprise or annoyance at an unannounced guest. I have the impression that she and her husband enjoy taking in strays and always have enough on hand to make guests feel welcome.

It had taken me a few minutes to reconcile the judge, with rolled up shirt sleeves and a tumbler of scotch, with the robed figure who presided over the hearing. Once we all got to talking, though, he became more animated and less judicial, just another person who wanted to talk about the Thorpe hearing. He seemed genuinely interested in my opinions, asking what I'd thought of some of the testimony.

"I realize how unpopular my decision is," he said at one point. "Believe me, I'm a Carlisle native just like all the spectators in that courtroom, and just like them, I'd hoped the testimony would lead to a different conclusion. But the law made my decision clear."

Until that moment, I hadn't thought much about Parker's personal feelings throughout the hearing, and I found his candor refreshing. A Thorpe fan, like all the rest of Carlisle. But one with the power to make life-altering decisions. What an awesome responsibility.

Since the judge was being so honest, I'd screwed up my nerve enough to say what had been on my mind all day.

"Your Honor, there's something that just doesn't sit right with me. Being in the courtroom every day, I really came to be on Thorpe's side, about as much as any of you who live here. And while I understand your decision, I can't help but feel that there's still some way, some how, that this might have ended differently.

"I'm certainly not questioning you," I continued cautiously, "but I can't stop thinking that there's more to this story."

The judge considered for a few moments, and then surprised me by saying, "Bud, I agree with you. Even in cases where the law leaves no room for doubt, human nature leaves plenty. I don't know of any judge who doesn't second guess himself at times, or worry that he's missed an important piece of information that might have led to a different verdict." He took a long sip of his drink before continuing, "We're supposed to be objective, but inside, we're just men who often can't help rooting for one side or the other."

As we continued to discuss the specifics of the Thorpe case, the judge made an interesting observation. "As I see it, the only way to restore Thorpe's medals was to grant him amateur status, and that could only be done if the AAU had known that he was paid to play baseball in Carolina. Knowingly granting him amateur status and then revoking it after the fact would certainly be grounds for a reversal. There was, however, no evidence of that."

I'd latched on to this statement, and carefully raised the possibility that there was more digging to be done. And lo and behold, by the end of the evening I'd left Pete's home with Judge Parker's blessing to pursue some research of my own. Before leaving town the following morning, I had an appointment to visit the judge's chambers to pick up copies of all the correspondence from the Thorpe hearing. I knew that on the train ride home, complaining about the heat would be the last thing on my mind.

In the two weeks since I got home to Harrisburg, I've spent most evenings poring over the hearing documents. In addition to the correspondence that Judge Parker gave me, my editor has also managed to secure copies of both the AAU and IOC regulations. The judge was certainly right—this is not light reading.

My editor, Jack O'Brien, is being cautiously optimistic about this project. He was pleased with my reporting on the hearing, and let me persuade him that the story isn't over. It's time consuming, though, and involves more research than I've ever done for a sports assignment. I never realized how rewarding it can be to investigate a story, searching for that one bit of information that can make a difference and, in this case, change a life.

I'm familiar with a good deal of the correspondence from the hearing, but I have found one interesting item that might be significant. There's a letter from Moses Friedman to the Commissioner of Indian Affairs, dated September 25, 1912, in which Friedman writes that Thorpe had turned down contract offers from a number of major league baseball teams in order to stay in school. Friedman also says that he advised Thorpe "to maintain his amateur standing, and not enter the ranks as a professional."

This was written three months after the Olympics, so if Thorpe was asking advice about professional offers at that time, it seems reasonable to conclude that he honestly considered himself an amateur. And obviously, so did Friedman.

Since I've gotten home, one line of Judge Parker's has been running through my mind almost continuously: "if the AAU had known that he was paid to play baseball in Carolina..." And why wouldn't they have known? Pop Warner submitted Thorpe's application in the fall of 1911, when Thorpe was already an accomplished football and track star who hoped to go to Stockholm. You'd think the AAU would have looked more closely at the backgrounds of athletes headed for the Olympics.

This afternoon, I reread all six of Johnson's articles about Thorpe. I needed a break from the IOC and AAU rule books and decided to start back at the beginning. I'd read them when they were published, of course, but at the time my anger at Johnson and Clancy clouded my perspective. And today, in the third piece, published on Sunday, January 26, 1913, I found something that made me sit up straight and take notice.

Johnson had reported that "James Sullivan was the head man at the American Sports Publishing Company on Warren Street in New York. The company that published Spaulding's baseball records, which tells of Thorpe's playing in the South on a team of which Charles Clancy of Stockbridge was manager."

Holy cow! Sullivan himself actually published the proof that Thorpe played ball in Carolina. So much has been made of whether Thorpe *knowingly* played as a professional and then *knowingly* competed as an amateur. Is it possible that Sullivan *knowingly* ignored

Thorpe's history until Clancy's revelation left him no choice but to acknowledge it?

I made this discovery at around 4:00 this afternoon. Though I had wanted to call Judge Parker and alert my editor, I needed more proof. And that's my goal now. I waited impatiently for everyone else to leave the newsroom, then brewed a pot of coffee and got to work.

Once I was alone, at about 6:30, I found the sports department's back copies of the Spaulding guide, just to see it for myself. It's hard to grasp Sullivan's actions. I guess his rationale was that, given Thorpe's talent and presumed success at the upcoming Olympics, having his rising star attached to the AAU could only benefit the organization. Yet another self-serving bureaucrat who took advantage of a vulnerable young man. But I still can't prove that he knew.

It's now after 10:00. The coffee's cold, I haven't eaten since lunch, but I just can't stop. I can feel how close I'm getting, and I'm afraid that if I quit now, I won't be able to get back to this same point tomorrow. Fortunately, this is Friday, so I don't have to be in the office in the morning—unless, of course, I'm still here, asleep at my desk.

Based on what Johnson reported about Sullivan, I had spent a couple of hours going over the AAU code book. But I struck out, and for the last hour or so I've been wading through the IOC regulations—again. Heaven knows, I've got Rule 26, the one that prohibits professional athletes from competing, memorized.

I know I'm missing something huge. Think, Murphy, think!

Reluctantly, I grab the IOC charter again. It's open to the index, and my eyes rest on the word grievances. What the hell, this whole case has become one big grievance.

I flip to that section and begin to read randomly. And in a passage of insignificant length but of significant consequence in the case of the 1912 Olympic Games, and one athlete in particular, I find what I've been looking for. I am physically trembling as I hold the book in my hands and read it a third, fourth, and fifth time, just to be sure.

Whatever Jim Thorpe did or didn't do, and whatever he did or didn't know, one fact is now abundantly clear. According to the IOC rules, any protest against an award must be lodged within thirty days from the closing ceremonies of the games. The V Olympiad ended on June 22, 1912. Roy Johnson's story ran on January 22, 1913. Seven months, to the very day—a full six months too late. I sit back slowly in my chair and think of Jim Thorpe and all he's been through. I know from talk after the hearing that he isn't granting any interviews or taking calls from the press, but he'll hear about this soon enough, and then, I suspect, I will be the one getting a phone call.

Anxious to call my editor with tomorrow's breaking headline news, I search for the phone buried under the stacks of reports and letters. This is sure to be the story of the year, the one I wanted to write all along. Next to the phone lies my trusty notebook, filled with interviews, reports, scratched out copy, headlines, and my observations and thoughts. As I flip through the pages, I smile at the memories, of a fancy hotel, a legendary coach, a king, an entire town and, of course, the world's greatest athlete, and a friendly desk clerk. On the first blank page, I write the headline for my story. "**IOC RULE MIGHT BE GOLDEN FOR THORPE**"

Underneath, I make one final note. Call Jimmy first thing in the morning.

EPILOGUE

On January 26, 1969, I volunteered to head up a committee for the Carlisle Jaycees. The goal of this committee was to have Jim Thorpe reinstated as the winner of the 1912 Olympic Pentathlon and Decathlon events. The effort was called "Project Jim Thorpe" and I spent three years gathering research, collecting facts, and finding out the truths behind why Jim Thorpe was removed as the winner of these 1912 Olympic events. During this time, my interest in Jim Thorpe became a passion as I was somehow reunited with the boy I remember from my past and was learning to respect this childhood hero all over again.

It was very clear to me, during the three years that I headed up the committee, that Jim Thorpe was a name that most people had heard of. Support came from all fifty states and beyond. Support came from the young and old, from members of Congress, and from State and local leaders.

I meet some great people, like Gus Welsh. He was Jim's roommate at the Carlisle Indian School, best man at Jim's wedding, and a member of the football team. Gus talked about Jim at length. He had always hoped that Jim's awards would be returned to him. He went on to say that he had tried for years to do what he could to have them returned.

Grace Thorpe, Jim's daughter, was always ready to help us with the project. While she was in Carlisle for the kick-off of Project Jim Thorpe, she gave me an insight to the famous Jim Thorpe. She said that her dad would say "Everyone is a lot more concerned than I am. What do I care for honors or awards. I would have liked to have kept the trophies, though."

Miss Thorpe went on to say, "Competing athletes knew Dad won the events. The whole world knew who was the only man to win both the decathlon and the pentathlon in the same year. Most important of all, Dad knew that he did it!"

Dealing with the Olympic organization was another matter. It became very clear that the Olympic organizations had no interest in Jim Thorpe nor in any type of reinstatement. It became "An Exercise in Frustration."

At one time I had asked Avery Brundage, President of the IOC, to have his organization, the International Olympic Committee, look into the reinstatement of Jim Thorpe. His reply in a letter to me was, "Jim Thorpe was only to have possession of the trophies until the next Games in 1916." Then he went on to say that I needed to direct any inquires to the international headquarters in Switzerland.

In a letter received from the United States Olympic Committee (USOC), the Executive Director noted, "All of the records from the IOC seem to support the charges levied against Mr. Thorpe. Quite frankly, this most recent request does not appear to have any chance of a hearing."

For three years it was "An Exercise in Frustration". The AAU would tell us that they could not help us and that we needed to contact the USOC. The USOC would tell us to contact the IOC. Around and around we went.

When it was all done, we had collected over a million signatures asking that the governing body review the Jim Thorpe case. With over a million signatures, the AAU, USOC and the IOC did not reply—we received not a word, just our registered mail receipt for all three organizations.

It was not until author-historian Robert W. Wheeler and his wife Florence Ridlon found the missing key to the Jim Thorpe reinstatement.

No one disputed that Thorpe had violated his amateur standing, but as Wheeler would persistently point out years later, there were many extenuating circumstances. In researching the bylaws of the 1912 Olympiad in the Library of Congress, for example, Ridlon uncovered the fact that "objections to the qualification of a competitor [must be] received by the Swedish Olympic Committee before the lapse of 30 days." The newspaper story that led to Thorpe's loss of amateur status didn't appear until six months after the Olympics.

Wheeler also reminded the IOC that it was the AAU, and not the IOC, that had originally ruled that Thorpe was a pro. The AAU changed its position on Thorpe in 1973, and the USOC did the same two years later. Wheeler argued that an IOC reversal should logically follow the AAU's. On October 13, 1982, the IOC Executive Committee approved Thorpe's reinstatement.

A question that remains in my mind, did the AAU know that the objections to the qualification had lapsed, or did they overlook the rules?

While doing research for this book, I came across a news story in the *New York Times*, dated Wednesday, January 29, 1913. This threw a whole new light on the subject.

THORPE ENTITLED TO PRIZES: Swedish Sportsman Says His Status Was Questioned Too Late.

STOCKHOLM, Jan. 28.—Swedish newspapers, commenting on the disclosure that James Thorpe was a professional athlete when he competed in the Olympic games held here last Summer, commended the honesty displayed by the Americans in making the fact known.

Leading authorities in the field of sport express the opinion that Thorpe is entitled to retain the prizes he won in the Pentathlon and Decathlon events, as his status as an amateur has been raised too late.

The Worcester Telegram, ran the same story on January 29, 1913, with the following headline:

SWEDEN FAVORS LETTING THORPE KEEP TROPHIES

Why a Historical Fiction?

First off, a historical fiction may center on historical characters, but represents an honest attempt based on considerable research to tell a story set in the historical past as understood by the author.

In my book, *A Hearing for Jim Thorpe*, the historical characters are used to tell a fiction hearing that was never provided to Jim Thorpe. In fact, the first story was released on January 22, 1913, and his awards were removed on January 29, 1913. In just seven short days and the AAU had completed the qualification process.

As an update, The Cumberland County Courthouse does still stand at the corner of Hanover and High Street in Carlisle, PA. The courtroom is on the second floor with county offices on the first floor. The courtroom is no longer used, but you can visit this historical building.

The Molly Pitcher Hotel was a "gem" to Carlisle, but today it is an apartment building for Senior Citizens.

Bud Murphy is a fictional character and is characterized much like the sport reporters of years past. *A Hearing for Jim Thorpe* would have been a circus, with reporters from around the world, just like an event today, where you'll find hundreds of TV satellite trucks sending back the story. In Bud Murphy's day, it was a reporter with a note pad.

Those were the good old days.

BIOGRAPHIES

Avery **Brundage** was an athlete, sports official, art collector, and philanthropist. A controversial figure, he has been widely criticized for attitudes expressed and decisions he made as a member of the United States Olympic Committee and as president of the International Olympic Committee.

Avery was an all-around athlete, competing in the 1912 Summer Olympics in Stockholm in the pentathlon and decathlon events, finishing 6th and 16th, respectively. He also won the US national all-around title in 1914, 1916, and 1918.

Charles Clancy was manager of the Winston-Salem baseball team of the Eastern Carolina League. It was reported by Roy Johnson, Sport Reporter for the *Worcester Telegram* newspaper, that Jim Thorpe played baseball for Charles Clancy. He stated that Jim Thorpe pitched and played first base for the Winston-Salem club in 1910.

Sister Katharine Drexel founded her own Catholic Order dedicated to working with and for the people she saw as America's forgotten, ignored, and debased peoples: Native Americans and African Americans. During her lifetime and under her leadership, the Sisters of the Blessed Sacrament built, funded, supplied, and staffed over sixty schools and missions throughout America.

Financially assisted by St. Katharine Drexel, she established a mission school at Saint Patrick Church for Blacks and Indians at the turn of the 20th century. Through the benevolence of St. Katharine Drexel, the current rectory was built originally as a convent and school.

Moses Friedman was Superintendent of the Carlisle Indian School.

Father Henry G. Ganss erected the present Saint Patrick Church, Carlisle, PA on 1893.

Father Ganss organized the Marquette League for Catholic Indian Missions in New York City as an auxiliary of the Society for the Preservation of the Faith among Indian Children.

Gustav V of Sweden was king of Sweden from 1907 to 1950.

The pentathlon trophy was a bronze bust of the King of Sweden, Gustav. King Gustav V, presented the trophy to Jim Thorpe on July 7, 1912. When presenting the trophy, he commented, "Sir, you are the greatest athlete in the world." Jim's reply was "Thanks, King."

Roy R. Johnson, Sport Reporter for the *Worcester Telegram* newspaper, was the reporter who released the front-page story about Jim Thorpe playing professional baseball in 1909 and 1910.

Margaret "Iva" Miller married Jim Thorpe on October 14, 1913, at Saint Patrick Church, Carlisle, PA.

At the age of 16, Iva arrived at the Carlisle Indian School on October 6, 1909 and left the school on June 24, 1912.

Richard Henry Pratt is best known as the founder and longtime superintendent of the influential Carlisle Indian Industrial School at Carlisle, Pennsylvania, where he profoundly shaped Indian education and federal Indian policy at the turn of the twentieth century.

He founded the Carlisle Indian Industrial School on November 1, 1879. This was the first of many non-reservation boarding schools for Native Americans. From 1879 to 1904, still on active military duty, Pratt directed the school, believing that the only way to save Indians from extinction was to remove Indian youth to non-reservation settings and then inculcate in them what he considered civilized ways. As head of the school, Pratt stressed both academic and industrial education.

Father Mark Stock was chaplain for the Catholic children at the Carlisle Indian School.

James Edward Sullivan was one of the founders of the Amateur Athletic Union (AAU) in 1888, serving as its secretary from 1889 until 1906 when he was elected as president of the AAU from 1906 to 1909. He declined a fourth term and was re-elected to his former position as secretary-treasurer until his sudden death.

His business career began in 1878 as a publisher. In 1880, he started the paper, *The Athletics News*. His career continued in sports publishing and the sporting goods businesses.

His athletics on the track had started in 1877 as a member of the Pastime Athletic Club. In 1888 and 1889 he won the all round championship of the club.

He also was one of the most influential people in the early Olympic movement, although his relationship with IOC president Pierre de Coubertin was tense.

Louis Tewanima was a member of the Carlisle Indian School Track Team and a teammate of Jim Thorpe. Louis competed mainly in the 10,000 meters.

He competed for United States in the 1908 Olympic Games, held in London, where he finished in ninth place in the Marathon. He also competed in the 1912 Summer Olympics held in Stockholm, Sweden, in the 10,000 meters where he won the silver medal.

James E. Thorpe reportedly began his athletic career at Carlisle in 1907 when he walked past the track and beat the school's high jumpers with an impromptu 5-ft. 9-in. jump while still wearing plain clothes. Track and Field were not the only events in which Thorpe engaged at Carlisle; he also participated in football, baseball, and lacrosse. Reportedly, Pop Warner was hesitant to allow Thorpe, his star track and field athlete, to compete in a physical game such as football. Thorpe, however, convinced Warner to let him run some plays against the school's defense; Warner assumed he would be tackled easily and give up the idea of playing football. Thorpe "ran around past and through them not once, but twice." He then walked over to Warner and said, "Nobody is going to tackle Jim," while flipping him the ball.

He gained nationwide attention for the first time in 1911. As a running back, defensive back, placekicker, and punter for his school's football team, Thorpe scored all of his team's points, four field goals and a touchdown in an 18–15 upset of Harvard. His team finished the season 11 to 1.

The following year, he led Carlisle to the national collegiate championship, scoring 25 touchdowns and 198 points. Carlisle's 1912 record included a 27–6 victory over Army. In that game, Thorpe scored a 92-yard touchdown that was nullified by a penalty incurred by a teammate; Thorpe then scored a 97-yard touchdown on the next play.

During that game, future President Dwight Eisenhower injured his knee while trying to tackle Thorpe. Eisenhower recalled of Thorpe in a 1961 speech, "Here and there, there are some people who are supremely endowed. My memory goes back to Jim Thorpe. He never practiced in his life, and he could do anything better than any other football player I ever saw." Thorpe was given All-American honors in both 1911 and 1912.

Football was and would remain Thorpe's favorite sport, and he competed only sporadically in track and field. Nevertheless, track and field would become the sport in which Thorpe would gain the most fame.

Glenn "Pop" Warner was born April 5, 1871, in Springville, New York. He attended Cornell University, where he graduated in 1894 with a law degree. At Cornell, Warner also played football. As captain of the football team, he got the nickname "Pop" because he was older than most of his teammates.

He coached at the Carlisle Indian School from 1899 to 1903, returned to Cornell University for three seasons, and then returned to Carlisle in 1907, the same year as Jim Thorpe arrived.

Gus Welch, a full-blood Chippewa born in Spooner, Wisconsin, was a member of the Carlisle Indian School Class of 1911, a quarterback for the Carlisle Indian School. Gus was a member of the U.S. track team for the 1912 Olympics (though illness prevented him from competing).

He gained notoriety in 1914 for his cooperation with a congressional investigation into the Carlisle Indian School management of the hefty sums of money the school handled.

He graduated from Dickinson School of Law in 1917.

Gus played professional football for the Canton, Ohio Bulldogs, coached by Jim Thorpe.

Father F. J. Welsh was pastor at Saint Patrick Church, Carlisle, PA. He assisted Father Mark Stock at the nuptial Mass for Jim Thorpe and Margaret Miller on October 14, 1913.

Point of Interest

1912 Olympic Games, officially known as the Games of the V Olympiad, were an international multi-sport event, which was celebrated in 1912 in Stockholm, Sweden. For the first time, competitors in the Games came from all five continents symbolized in the Olympic rings. Also for the first time since 1896, all athletic events were held from May 5 to July 22. It was the last time that solid gold medals were awarded; modern medals are usually gold plated silver.

Amateur Athletic Union (AAU) is one of the largest, non-profit, volunteer, sports organizations in the United States. A multi-sport organization, the AAU is dedicated exclusively to the promotion and development of amateur sports and physical fitness programs.

"The AAU was founded in 1888 to establish standards and uniformity in amateur sport. During its early years the AAU served as a leader in international sport representing the United States in the international sports federations. The AAU worked closely with the Olympic movement to prepare athletes for the Olympic Games.

Carlisle Indian School was founded in 1879 by Richard Henry Pratt. The school was the first off-reservation government boarding school for Native American Indian children. Carlisle served as the model for dozens of schools throughout the U.S., some of which are still in existence.

The United States Army War College now occupies the site of the former school.

Carlisle, Pennsylvania, is the county seat for Cumberland County and was settled in 1751 and incorporated in 1782. Dickinson College, a liberal arts college chartered in 1783, just a few days after the American Revolution ended with the treaty of Paris as the first college of the new United States of America. Carlisle was the home of the Carlisle Indian School.

Eastern Carolina League was a minor league baseball affiliation which operated in the Eastern part of North Carolina. The league operated from 1908 to 1910 It was classified as a class "D" league.

By far, the most famous person to come out of the league was Jim Thorpe. Some consider Thorpe the greatest athlete of the twentieth century. It was his involvement with the Eastern Carolina League that cost him his amateur status and his Olympic medals.

Jim Thorpe played for Rocky Mount and Fayetteville, NC during the summers of 1909 and 1910.

International Olympic Committee (IOC) is an organization based in Lausanne, Switzerland, created on June 23, 1894. Its membership consists of the 205 National Olympic Committees.

The IOC organizes the modern Olympic Games held in Summer and Winter, every four years. The first Summer Olympics organized by the International Olympic Committee was held in Athens, Greece, in 1896; the first Winter Olympics was held in Chamonix, France, in 1924. Until 1992, both Summer and Winter Olympics were held in the same year. After that year, however, the IOC shifted the Winter Olympics to the even years between Summer Games, to help space the planning of the two events two years apart from one another.

Saint Patrick Church traces its history to Revolutionary times, forming a congregation in 1779 and is the first church in America named in honor of Ireland's patron saint. The first church was a log structure built in 1784, and a brick church was erected on the present site in 1806. That building gave way to a new foundation designed and erected by Father Henry Ganss and was dedicated in 1894. A fire in 1923 destroyed most of the building and the present church was rebuilt within one year.

Jim Thorpe and Margaret (Iva) Miller were married at Saint Patrick Church on October 14, 1913. Father Mark Stock, chaplain for the Catholic children at the Carlisle Indian School, performed the ceremony, assisted by Father F. J. Welsh, pastor of Saint Patrick Church.

A teammate of Jim Thorpe, Gus Welch, was the best man at the wedding.

United States Olympic Committee (USOC) began as a small group, headed by James E. Sullivan, the founder of the Amateur Athletic Union, which entered United States athletes in the inaugural Modern Olympic Games in Athens in 1896. Dr. William Milligan Sloane served as the first president of the committee in 1894. The formal committee, initially named the American Olympic Association, was formed at a meeting in November 1921 at the New York Athletic Club.

The United States Olympic Committee, one of America's premier sports organizations, is headquartered in Colorado Springs, Colo.

Worcester Telegram is a daily newspaper in Worcester, Massachusetts.

In late January 1913, the *Worcester Telegram* published stories announcing that Thorpe had played professional baseball. The story broke on the front page of the *Worcester Telegram* of Wednesday, January 22, 1913. The headline "THORPE WITH PROFESSIONAL BASEBALL TEAM SAYS CLANCY" was on the front page. The second headline "Manager of Winston-Salem Outfit in Carolina Association, in Southbridge for winter, Tells of Indian Athlete's Diamond Career."

The newspaper charge was based on the statement of Charles Clancy, manager of the Winston-Salem baseball team of the Eastern Carolina League. Clancy was quoted as stating that the Indian pitched and played first base for the Winston-Salem club in 1910.